SIX-GUN
CROSSROAD

SIX-GUN CROSSROAD

Lauran Paine

BLACK STONE PUBLISHING

Copyright © 2016 by Lauran Paine Jr.

Published in 2018 by Blackstone Publishing

Printed in the United States of America

ISBN 978-1-4708-6105-6

Fiction / Westerns

1 3 5 7 9 10 8 6 4 2

CIP data for this book is available
from the Library of Congress

Blackstone Publishing
31 Mistletoe Rd.
Ashland, OR 97520

www.BlackstonePublishing.com

CHAPTER ONE

In most ways Sam Logan was nondescript. He didn't stand more than five feet eight inches and in heft he didn't top the scales at more than 160 pounds. If that was not insignificant enough he was gray over the ears, probably was forty or better in age, and dressed like any other range rider, with the possible exception that Sam's .45 had a mother-of-pearl handle.

Most men were content to wear their .45s with the black rubber stocks that came from the factory. A few, usually young buckaroos full of swagger and vinegar, saved up and got handsome ivory butts. Now and then a rider came down the line with a carved walnut grip on his six-gun. But the men who sported genuine mother-of-pearl handles were rare.

Still, beautiful grips on a man's gun didn't make him one inch taller or an inch broader. They didn't make him handsome if nature hadn't so endowed him, and they surely couldn't peel off a single one of those forty-odd years, so Sam remained just another drifter, but with a mite more age on him than most drifters had. That warm and fragrant June afternoon he came along the westward trace into Ballester, Utah Territory, a few years after the last Indian scuffle, a few years before the steam cars came panting into the territory, and actually into a sort of deep vacuum between what had once been and what was not quite yet.

Sam's hundred and sixty was well proportioned. His arms were thick and powerful, his shoulders heavy, his chest deep. His face was open and candid and there was a little humorous lilt to his wide-lipped mouth. He was one of those men who seem so very ordinary that folks scarcely looked at him twice, and toward whom they warmed at once without any reservations. Sam Logan had made his share of enemies through life, but rarely had it been necessary for him to make them if he'd only stepped aside now and then. But that wasn't like Sam Logan. He had his ideals and his convictions, and did not compromise with either.

Still, in Ballester, folks accepted him as just another cowboy. In springtime every town got its share of them, mostly restless after the enforced restrictions of a cold winter. They were mostly gregarious and generous, and sometimes a little raw around the edges, but that wore off after they got work and sweated out their pent-up meanness. Yet when Sam Logan killed two men in a little more than twenty-four hours after his arrival in Ballester, that made a difference.

Not, as folks said, that the killings weren't justified. Neither of those men was popular around Ballester and both, so said the bartender up at the Golden Slipper Saloon, were surly, brutish men. But still, killings shocked folks, worried them, made them a little indignant and a lot uneasy. If line riders could drift into a place and shoot folks down, there was no telling who was safe or what this dratted world was coming to. So, because Sam Logan was also a stranger in town, people began to eye him askance and mention to the deputy sheriff stationed at Ballester that, justified or not, maybe Sam ought to be told to move along.

No doubt the worst part of it was that none of the cattle outfits would hire Sam. He sat over in front of the livery barn and endlessly whittled, or else he sat up at the Golden Slipper upon a tilted-back chair in a gloomy corner, his hat pushed back, his feet a foot off the floor, and sipped beer.

He still smiled easily, though, when folks nodded or spoke as they passed by, still appeared as friendly as a mongrel pup. But once a man has killed in a town folks can't forget it. Regardless of what other virtues a man might display, before or after, it was always the killings people remembered. Moreover, as time passed and Sam made no attempt to ride on but became instead almost a permanent fixture on the bench in front of the livery barn, or up at the Golden Slipper, mothers told their children to use the opposite side of the road. Tough cowhands from the outlying ranches stepped widely around Sam, and the liveryman himself told the deputy that Sam was ruining his business, sitting out there on his bench whittling those darned fool little dolls all the time.

How the killings had come about was simple. Sam, being a lot less than a six-footer, received the easy and condescending treatment big powerful men usually reserved for lesser men. He was at the bar one afternoon hiding from the sun, which got really hot in Ballester in June, when a Snowshoe cowboy named Forrest Banning had come in to take on a load of buffalo sweat. Forrest was a good-natured enough man unless he'd been drinking. By 5:00 he wasn't good-natured and he wasn't drinking. He'd decided, for some reason no one ever found out, that he resented Sam Logan, standing down the bar from him. He didn't like Sam's mother-of-pearl pistol grips. He didn't like Sam's easy, pleasant look, and he particularly didn't like Sam's less than magnificent size. Twice the barman had told Forest he'd better get on back to the Snowshoe, and twice Forrest had told the barman to mind his own business. The third time Forrest had spoken it had been to Sam. He said disagreeably that he'd once known a dance-hall girl over in Kansas who'd used mother-of-pearl on her garters, and it seemed to him that no man worth being called one would use the stuff—unless, of course, he was more woman than man.

Sam hadn't gotten angry then, as the bartender had later stated at the coroner's hearing. He'd simply smiled and offered to buy Forrest Banning a drink.

Forrest had then said he wouldn't be caught dead drinking with a man who lived off cheap women, and that, related the barman, had done it. Sam stopped smiling and gazed for a long time at Forrest. Finally he said: "Cowboy, the trouble with you is that you can't drink. I reckon you'd better do like the barman told you a while back … get out of here."

Forrest had then let off a bawl like a bravo bull, had jumped clear of the bar, and had gone for his gun. There were not, according to the barman, any other patrons in the saloon at the time; it was too late for the morning drunks and too early for the drinkers at day's end. So the only one around to duck had been the barman himself. That, he explained, was how he had come not to witness the actual shooting. He dropped down behind the bar and heard a gunshot—just one. He'd remained out of sight until Sam Logan had quietly told him it was all right, he could stand up again. He did, he told the court, and looked over his bar, and there lay Forrest Banning with that purple-puckered little hole between his eyes as dead as a post and flat on his back.

Had Forrest drawn his gun? the judge asked. All the bartender could say was that the .45 was out of Forrest's holster on the floor. It could have been drawn out or it could have fallen out when Banning hit the floor. But of one thing that barman was dead certain. Forrest Banning had never gotten to fire it. This, the deputy sheriff later averred from the same chair at the hearing, was the truth. Banning's gun hadn't been fired.

The barman undoubtedly had told the pure truth. Just as undoubtedly he had saved Sam Logan's life.

The second killing had been two days after the first one. In a way, so the deputy had philosophized at the second hearing, it was a predictable killing. When asked to elaborate on that interesting statement, he had said that when a man like Forrest Banning was killed, since he was an ordinary cowboy and had usually his share of friends, there was predictably at least one of them who was a partner to the dead man, either on the trail or around the branding fires, and this partner, after a day or two of grief and brooding, could often be counted upon to ride in and seek out his friend's killer.

It was this statement as well as the circumstances surrounding that second killing that saved Sam Logan the second time.

He had been sitting in the morning sun over in front of the livery barn when Vestal Johnson had ridden in from the Snowshoe range with his gun tied down and murder in his eyes. Most folks around Ballester had encountered Vestal a time or two. He'd been a steady hand out at Snowshoe for over a year. He was a quiet, distant kind of man, neither more nor less friendly whether he'd been drinking or whether he was stone sober. The men liked him the way they liked any other top hand. It was actually more a matter of respect for a fast rope, a light rein hand, a steady grip on the hot iron, than any equation of warmth toward an individual. Some of the subpoenaed cowboys even said Vestal was surly and easily roiled, but mostly the range men simply shrugged and stated that Vestal was just another pretty good cowboy.

But being a pretty good cowboy wasn't nearly enough the morning he dismounted in front of the livery barn in plain sight of the whole town, looped his reins at the tie rack, stepped away from the horse, and made a slow, meticulous study of Sam Logan, over where Sam was diligently carving with his Barlow knife in the pleasant morning sunlight.

Sam said he'd seen the rider come up and get down, but he also said he hadn't paid any attention because he was carving a particularly fine model of a Morgan stud horse for one of the kids around town and had been very engrossed in his work.

Then Vestal had said: "Shorty, get up from there."

Twenty solemn witnesses including seven woman shoppers

who had been passing nearby at the time, recalled those exact words under oath. They also recalled how Sam Logan had slowly raised his head and gazed out where Vestal Johnson had taken his stand, some ten or fifteen feet to the right of his tethered Snowshoe horse.

"What for?" Sam had asked.

"Because," Vestal had said, adding to it a fighting designation that cast doubts upon Sam's legitimacy, "you done shot a good friend of mine when he was too drunk to help hisself. That's why, you yellow damned whelp … *now get up from there!*"

Abner Fuller, the liveryman, recounted under oath what had happened next. He had been loafing just inside the doorless opening to his barn, and until Vestal called Sam Logan that name, he hadn't really thought there was going to be trouble. Afterward, he related, he'd been too petrified to move. Sometimes, he stated, the slightest movement caused men to draw and fire at a shadow when they were keyed up to it. He'd stood there sweating a river and hoping against all hope Sam Logan would figure some way to wiggle out of having to fight.

But Sam hadn't. He'd closed his Barlow knife, put it carefully into a pocket, leaned over without arising from the chair to place the wooden horse he'd been whittling on out of harm's way, then he'd straightened back up—still making no move to stand up—and studied Vestal Johnson a minute. "You better forget it," he'd said, speaking very distinctly and quietly. "Your pardner forced that fight. I didn't even know him. I don't know you either, and I sure don't want to kill you."

Vestal called Logan that name again, Abner Fuller related, then, with Abner's eyes straight on him, Vestal had dropped his right shoulder, arm and hand straight down. Sam dropped off the end of the bench, hit the dirt, rolled half over, and was firing his mother-of-pearl .45 before he'd even stopped rolling. Vestal took two of those slugs head on. One in the brisket that knocked him backward six or eight feet with its frightful impact, and the second one through the head before he hit the ground. His hat flew all the way across the road and landed up against the far plank walk where some men were standing. Those men, Abner said, seemed to explode. They ran in every direction.

"And …?" the judge had prompted Abner.

"Well, sir … Your Honor … I couldn't hardly believe me eyes. That short feller got off both of them shots before Vestal even got his gun out, and believe me when I sit right here and tell you … sir, Your Honor … his damned fingers was closing around the Forty-Five's butt before this here Sam Logan even flung himself off my bench."

Other witnesses, less observant, farther away, or unwilling to state what they'd plainly seen because no one would ever believe them, only stated that they'd seen Sam Logan shoot and Vestal Johnson hit the ground.

That was the end of the inquiry into the second killing—that of Snowshoe's rider, Vestal Johnson. Twenty witnesses had solemnly trooped up to the witness chair, been sworn in, and had candidly told how they'd seen Vestal ride up and deliberately provoke Sam Logan into a gunfight. The outcome of both the hearing and the gunfight was salutary for Sam Logan.

Two weeks later he was still over in front of Abner Fuller's livery barn, carving things with his Barlow knife, and the town of Ballester was in a quiet turmoil because no one knew what to do about it. Not even the deputy sheriff to whom everyone protested and complained and grumbled.

CHAPTER TWO

Percy Whittaker was one inch under six feet tall but weighed close to a couple hundred pounds. He was one of those men whose breadth made him sometimes look a yard taller than he was. Perc had been a cowboy for seven years before he took up the deputy's job at Ballester. He didn't know much legal law but he knew his share of common-sense law. He'd wade into a cage of lions bare-handed or a brawling clutch of range riders, there wasn't much difference. He had a punch that could break a jaw or, aimed lower, could put a man on a boiled milk diet for a week.

The folks of Ballester both liked and respected Perc. The cattlemen respected him, too, but did not always like him. For one thing, having been a cowboy himself, he knew exactly when a big blow-off was coming and would be there to put a damper on things. He was a tolerant man, good-natured and even, and it was hinted a mite lazy. What folks around Ballester were beginning to learn was that this combination made the best peace officer.

Percy Whittaker was less than thirty years of age. He'd never said how much less and folks hadn't really cared enough to inquire. He had gray eyes and brown hair, a sort of perpetual pucker around the eyes and a square, thrusting iron jaw. He was good with the .45

he wore, but, although he'd been stationed in Ballester several years, he'd never shot anyone.

Not that Ballester was a quiet town. It wasn't, not with the big Snowshoe outfit west of town, the Rainbow outfit—sometimes called the Big Half Circle—north of town, and the Mexican Hat outfit east of town. In places where there were immigrants and considerable through travel, trouble usually came in small unrelated doses, maybe a shooting over a card game or an argument at a tie rack, or maybe some imagined insult in the roadway. Isolated instances beyond the mainstream of orderly existence that lawmen handled with such dispatch that frequently most of a town's residents didn't even know there'd been trouble.

But in a place like Ballester it was different. The town itself sat squarely in the middle of nowhere. It had grown slowly from an old-time trading post into what it now was simply because the big cattle outfits had grown up around it, making it their hub for supplies and recreation. Ballester had no other earthly reason for existence. If Snowshoe and Rainbow and Mexican Hat had moved on or folded up or curtailed their expansive operations, Ballester would have withered on the vine.

The stage road passed through, true enough, but rarely indeed did any one alight at Ballester except salesmen—called drummers—plying their trade among the local stores and merchants, or some cowboy lugging a saddle and bedroll and looking for employment.

Therefore, when trouble erupted in Ballester, everyone was in some way and to some degree involved. Those killings by Sam Logan, for example, had Abner Fuller sweating bullets. As he'd complained bitterly to Percy Whittaker, Sam sitting in front of his livery barn, day in and day out, was hurting his trade. Folks didn't enjoy passing a killer every time they wished to hire a hack or rent a horse.

The proprietor of the Golden Slipper Saloon, Everett Champion, a raw-boned old miserly type in his sixties who watered his whiskey and, it was rumored, stacked his card decks, told Perc that while

Sam's presence in the Slipper didn't actually hurt trade—it even seemed sometimes to make it better because men rode in from miles around to get a look at the fellow with the mother-of-pearl gun grips—it nevertheless made Everett feel uncomfortable, having Logan perched back there in the shadows on his tipped-back chair, watching everything Everett did.

There were some other complaints, too. For example, Johnny West, range boss for the Snowshoe outfit, rode into town to arrange for the planting of Vestal Johnson, as he'd also done for Forrest Banning, and he told Perc that his men were aggravated by Logan's presence. Every time they rode into town, there he was, either sitting in front of the barn when they went across to put up their horses, or perched on that chair in the shadows up at the Slipper.

Johnny West was a thick-set, nut-brown, hard-working man who said exactly what he meant, always, and was primarily loyal to the outfit that paid his wages. His men liked him and Perc Whittaker did, too, which was more than could be said of other range bosses around the country. But then Johnny never threw his weight around just because he bossed a big crew of riders, or because his word was law on ten thousand acres of land. The Snowshoe outfit was owned by a syndicate of Denver businessmen. It ran a lot of cattle, a large crew of top hands, and was a good money-maker. It also spent a sizeable sum every year in Ballester so the merchants always listened when its representative—Johnny West—spoke.

Perc listened, too, but for a different reason. He'd once worked for West out at Snowshoe. In fact, that had been his last cowpunching job before signing on as resident deputy in town, so when Johnny appeared at the jailhouse the day he made arrangements for Vestal Johnson's burial with his complaints against Sam Logan, Perc sat and listened and was sympathetic. But he was also non-committal.

"There's no law against him hanging around town," he told Johnny West. "As long as he doesn't make trouble."

"Well, hell," stated the husky range boss, "isn't two killings trouble?"

"Johnny, *he* didn't make that trouble. Forrest and Vestal made it. A man's got every right under the law, as I see it, to defend himself."

"All right," said Johnny West, taking another approach to the same problem. "He's not good for the town. Look at old Everett or listen to Ab Fuller. Go through the stores ... the saddle shop, the emporium, the café, the smithy, they all say Logan's poison around here."

Perc dropped his head and looked glum. He'd heard all those complaints first-hand, and still, Sam Logan didn't bother folks. He sat and whittled, drank a little beer, and had his bedroll out beyond town somewhere in one of the old abandoned shacks.

"He's waiting for work, Johnny, that's all. When someone hires him, he'll pull out of town."

Johnny snorted. "Who'd hire him? I sure wouldn't. I *couldn't*. If I was going to die tomorrow unless I hired him on, I wouldn't dass do it. Why, the way my riders feel right now, they'd blow a hole in him you could drive a four-up hitch through. And the other outfits ... they've all heard about him. Perc, no one's going to hire Logan. No one. Not if he sits around here for a year. He's poison any way you look at him. You got to find some way to get rid of him."

Perc had remained non-committal. Johnny had gone back to Snowshoe after paying Doc Farraday for Vestal Johnson's burial, and Sam Logan still sat and whittled and waited, seemingly unaware that everyone around him was to some extent or some degree involved in his two killings.

Two more weeks passed and no one had hired Sam Logan. The kids around town adored him. He carved them wooden guns and miniature horses and stalwart Indians that he colored with the juice of chokecherries he got down near the creek east of town. Abner Fuller was at his wit's end. He'd never actually suggested to Sam that he find some other place to sit and do his whittling. The bald fact was that Ab was not and had never been a really courageous man. He'd had a fight or two in his earlier years but never with guns and never with anyone at all if he could avoid it.

He had gotten in the habit, however, when business was particularly slack, of going outside and standing near the bench where Sam loafed, to watch the carving. As he later told Perc Whittaker, he'd never in his life seen a man with so much natural talent in his hands.

"It's a real gift, Perc. He carved a cowboy sitting his horse with a wind at his back and I swear I could almost feel the cold blast on my own back, the way that fellow was hunched up and shivering."

"Shivering?" said Perc. "A carving, shivering, Ab?"

"Well. You know what I mean. It's so danged realistic you can *feel* that fellow shivering up there atop his head-hung horse. I tell you, Logan's got a real gift in them hands of his."

"Yeah," agreed the deputy, "he's got a gift in his hands, all right." Perc wasn't thinking of carving, though. He was thinking how fast with a gun a man would have to be to put bullets into the heads of two men who were already drawing on him before he even went for his own gun.

Then, on a golden Saturday in July with the first promise of real summertime heat in the air but with the air still as clear as glass and as fragrant as only cow-country air could be, one of those itinerant preachers rolled into Ballester with an askew stovepipe sticking up from the top of his wagon, and being drawn along by a pair of old pelters Noah must have had on the ark, they were so old.

He had a big bushy beard the color of salt on pepper, a wild thatch of tousled hair to match, had to be in his late fifties, and had a pair of hard blue eyes that went through anyone he looked at. He said his name was Parson Jonah Reeves and his daughter's name was Abigail, that he'd heard of the iniquities of Ballester, and had driven all the way from Wolf Hole, Arizona, to give battle to the devil in these parts, or, as he thundered to Perc Whittaker and Ab Fuller at the livery barn where he sought parking space for his rig, in these last days he would wrestle Satan for the salvageable souls in this den of evil and sinful iniquity.

Perc had looked and listened and said nothing. Ab had shown Parson Reeves a spot near the community corral where he might park his outfit, then Ab had come back and had asked Perc just what in tarnation "salvageable souls" were? Perc replied that he thought Parson Reeves meant folks who hadn't gone off the deep end and committed sins that couldn't really be forgiven.

Abner had thought that over and had then stated that in his opinion, although he didn't know for a fact much about the degrees of sin, he felt reasonably certain that Parson Reeves had his work cut out for him in Ballester.

Perc hadn't felt disposed to debate the point. Those sky pilots came and went. Another one had passed through three years earlier, and he had almost gotten the folks to raise up a church. But in the end he'd said the offerings just didn't quite suffice and had driven on—with the offerings.

This one, though, struck Perc as being quite different from the run-of-the-mill. For one thing, aside from his piercing eyes and wild whiskers, he was as thick as oak and twice as strong. He wasn't six feet tall but he weighed about two hundred and ten, had arms and legs like tree trunks, and when he spoke it was like distant cannon fire. He didn't strike Perc as the type of man who'd always been a preacher. Unless Perc was very badly mistaken, there was a knife scar under his right ear that ran down his cheek into his beard, and one of his thick, brawny hands had a shiny place where the hair did not grow, exactly the shape of an old bullet scar.

Abigail was quite different. She was small and sturdily put together with curves in places where most womenfolk didn't even have places. She looked to be maybe thirty or a year or two under thirty. Her eyes were as blue as cornflowers, her hair was a subdued golden brown, and her lips were full and curving. Also, she wore a thin golden wedding band on her marrying finger, so she either had a husband somewhere or else she was a widow. But there was no mistaking one thing. Jonah Reeves was her pappy. Aside from their common solidness of build, their jaws and eyes and mannerisms were identical.

Abigail was old Jonah's daughter, all right, and that was a relief to Perc Whittaker because in Ballester the womenfolk, like womenfolk everywhere else, had a way of sniffing and probing and slyly gossiping. Nothing was sacred to them either, maybe with good reason, for men were men, even men of the cloth, and since they were married females, like Ab's wife for instance, they had reason to know how it went with men. Healthy men anyway.

The day after Parson Reeves hit town was a Sunday.

Normally the menfolk congregated up at the Slipper in a comfortable atmosphere of tobacco and horse sweat and whiskey to play poker or gossip or drink. No stages passed through town on Sunday and until early afternoon only a few cowhands appeared in town, so things, ordinarily at least, were drowsy and peaceful and comfortable. Perc usually didn't bother making a round of the town Sunday mornings. He had a room over at the boarding house where he sat around or read the week-old newspapers, or listened to the drummers who'd been caught in Ballester and couldn't depart until the stage came through on Monday.

The womenfolk sometimes met at someone's house for an impromptu prayer meeting, after which they sewed and gossiped or went straight home to start preparing the big Sunday midday meal.

It was all pre-ordained. Maybe some of it didn't exactly jibe with the wishes or the desires of the people, but traditionally that's how Sundays were spent in Ballester, had been spent for a long time, so no one ever really departed from this comfortable ritual. At least they hadn't up to the time Sam Logan arrived in town, and for a few weeks after he'd arrived, until Jonah Reeves had arrived.

Perc Whittaker was at the boarding house, talking to a beef buyer from Denver. There was a growing demand throughout the Midwest for grassed-out steers, the buyer was saying. Since the slump of a few years back, which had broken the back of the Texas trade, few trail herds had been coming over the plains to Kansas and Nebraska, while at the same time, so the buyer stated, the emigrant settler growth of the same region had pushed up the beef demand until packers, slaughterers, and canners were sending commission men as far West as Utah, and even Idaho, for meat on the hoof delivered down in Kansas.

All this was interesting. It was also soporific and Perc was on the verge of dozing off in his chair when Ab Fuller rushed in from the roadway, calling insistently for the law. Perc looked at Ab's distraught face and heaved up to his feet, sure there'd been another killing.

"He's ruining the saloon," Ab gasped. "Perc, you got to come at once, that bushy-faced old coot's ruining the saloon!"

CHAPTER THREE

Perc heard that unmistakable cannon-roll voice long before he and Ab got up to the Golden Slipper. "Be not deceived. God is not mocked, for whatsoever a man soweth, that shall he also reap!"

Ab also heard it. He said: "See, what'd I tell you. Perc, you never saw the likes of it."

Whittaker turned and reached for the batwing doors as he said: "Saw what, Abner?"

"Look in there," the liveryman whispered, hanging back to let Perc enter first. "Just look in there."

Perc stepped inside and halted. Behind him Abner kept saying in his fading whisper: "See. Look there. He's ruined the place. See."

There stood the Parson Reeves in the middle of the saloon, his hair standing out in every direction, his frizzled big beard tangled, his coat off and his shirt torn, his huge fists balled up, and his fierce eyes sparking like pale lightning.

There were at least ten men lined up down the bar with their backs to it and another ten, including three prone cowboys, scattered among the tables and over along the roadside wall. In his customary place, tilted up and nursing a 5¢ glass of beer, sat Sam Logan, looking as startled, as entirely unnerved, as everyone else who was looking.

Even seasoned old saloonkeeper Everett Champion was not saying a word. Upon a nearby upended poker table the parson's coat had been carefully folded and put aside. The day bartender was leaning across his counter with a sawed-off shotgun in his hands, but he hadn't cocked the weapon and wasn't holding it like he truly meant to use it.

With those three sprawled range riders scattered like cast-aside dolls around him, Jonah Reeves thundered his denunciations and his scorching invective, raising mighty arms on high and rolling his fierce old eyes like a prophet of old.

"And He cometh to this place of sinfulness and cast out the devils, and He departed and sent in His place His servant, Jonah Reeves, to smite the Philistine thigh and jaw, to bring down the idols in shambles, to put into the people His spirit and His tenderness."

Reeves dropped his arms. He turned and glared. He drew back a mighty breath and roared at them, driving them deeper into their awed silence.

"And ye mock Him. Ye drink strong waters on His day and sit in lust with cards in your unclean hands. Ye smoke up this place with your filthy tobacco and ye squander His day in evil-doing. And He sent me to warn you. He will not be mocked. He *shall not* be mocked! Ye will listen to His word on the Sabbath and walk in His ways. Ye will lift up thine eyes from the evilness of your daily lives and praise Him unto the last man ... in these last days!"

Perc stood and looked. Everett Champion caught his eye and silently beseeched Perc to do something. Perc did. He walked forward and stopped a long arm's distance away. It was hard to look into those flaming eyes, into that agitated face, and not feel like bracing into the older man's towering earnestness.

"And you," Jonah Reeves thundered, pointing an oaken arm at Perc Whittaker, speaking in a roar that made the windows shudder. "What have you done to preserve His law? What have you done in this Sodom on the plains to exalt His way? I'll tell you ... nothing! Nothing at all! Well, Deputy, let me tell you ... God has come to Ballester in Utah Territory. He came up out of the desert to you in these highlands, he dispatched His faithful servant, Jonah Reeves, to win you from your wickedness, to teach you brotherly love and prayer and humility. And Jonah Reeves will show you the way even if he has to take you by the scruff of the neck and the seat of your britches, for there be none so blind as those who will not see! Hereafter this saloon, this vipers' den, this stinking hole of brimstone, will close on the Sabbath, and there will be prayer meetings in Ballester at my wagon until we can find a better place for His good works. You remember that. After this no saloon will be open for trade on His day!" Reeves paused to suck back another big breath before he could roar on.

Perc spoke up: "Parson, what happened to these three cowboys on the floor?"

Reeves looked down as though from a great height, as though he couldn't recall immediately what had happened. Then he lost some of his irate stiffness, flexed his battered knuckles, and said: "Oh, yes, those men. Deputy, they attempted to dispute with His servant, Jonah Reeves. That tall one there with the Snowshoe brand burned into his vest … that one came at me full of strong waters and profanity to heave me out of Satan's house. I cracked him alongside the ear. Them other two … they came at me together, the pair of them. I laid the first one down with a chop to the back of the head and crushed the second one's wind out."

Everett Champion at long last found his voice. But even so he didn't sound nearly as wrathful as he should have sounded, so Perc gazed curiously over across at him.

"Perc, he downed 'em just like he said," old Champion stated, jumping his gaze from Perc to Jonah and back again. "He didn't have no gun on so they went to throw him out by hand."

"Doesn't look like they did so good," murmured Perc, eyeing the unconscious men. "What'd he hit 'em with?"

"His fists," a man over by the door said in quiet awe. "I heard the strike when he downed that first one ... that long-legged Snowshoe man. I swear I thought he'd crushed the rider's skull. Sounded like someone kicking a pumpkin. Soggy and sort of crunching like."

Perc lifted his head and steadily stared at Jonah Reeves. "Parson, you can't go around fighting folks in this town. And look at that poker table and those chairs. They've all got busted legs. You'll owe Everett for that."

Reeves raised his shoulders and expanded his powerful chest. He was taking in one of those big lungs full of air that seemed to characterize him just before he roared and bellowed and set the windows to rattling. Perc hurried to head him off.

"Hold it, Parson. Wait a minute now. I'm not through. We've got laws in Ballester against disturbing the peace. Sunday in this town is a day of rest."

"But not reverence!" thundered the parson. "Rest and wickedness, Deputy, but not reverence and repentance!"

"Well. What folks do with their free times is their own business so long as they don't ..."

"Their own business! Hah, look around you, Deputy. Look at their dissipated faces, at their watery eyes, at the loose and lustful lips. Sin is amongst them I tell you! Sin and wickedness and immorality! Look at them, I say! Look at their wasted faces!"

"Parson, tone it down a little. No one's deaf in here."

"Deaf? You're all deaf to the Word of the Lord. And you're blind, too ... but His servant, Jonah Reeves, has arrived amongst you to wrestle with the imps of Satan for your battered souls. Never fear, boys, from this Sunday on we'll join in the good fight." Reeves turned, caught up his coat, flung it high around his head once like a saintly banner, and turned to march majestically on across the room toward the door. "Repent," he rumbled. "Repent, sinners. Take heed of your evil ways! Look ye to His servant, Jonah Reeves, for your eternal salvation. Raise up thine eyes on high to His mansions in the sky. Meet next Sunday at my wagon and get your absolution."

He passed on out into the balmy afternoon sunlight and Perc, moving closer to look past the doors, saw Abigail come up and stop. "Father," she said, "supper's about ready."

"Yes, child, yes," Jonah said, rolling down his sleeves and throwing the coat across his massive shoulders. "I've a good appetite. Verily I tell you, Abbie, I've need for meat and potatoes. In this town the devil lurks everywhere. It's going to take a long time to heave him out. I'll need my strength and my convictions. Come along now, let's go tell Him the good word ... that we've arrived and have joined battle with Mephisto."

They walked away down through the dozing golden-lit roadway side-by-side, turned in over at Ab's barn, and passed around toward the public corral.

Abner touched Perc's arm. "None of these boys is named Mephisto," he said. "That one's named Clark, that one's called Jerry Something-Or-Other, and that big one's a Rainbow rider but I can't quite lay my tongue to his name. It'll come to me, though, in a ..."

"What," asked Perc of the roomful of stationary and stunned men, "exactly happened in here?"

It was Sam Logan, back there in his gloomy place upon his tipped-back chair, who answered first. "He came through those spindle doors like a bravo bull, his arms up and his eyes looking wild and his whiskers standing straight out in front of him. He let out a bawl you could've heard to Salt Lake City and upended that poker table, scattering cards and chips and men like tenpins. He started over to clean out the bar, too, I think, but that long-legged cowboy there turned and rushed him. That old devil rolled clear of two punches and laid bone up against that cowboy's head like he was pole axing a steer. Down that one went. The other two rushed him next." Logan shook his head. "Damnedest thing I ever saw." He added nothing to that.

Around the room voices began to mumble, to lift and strengthen and rush all together. Men began relating what they'd just seen as though they'd been the only ones in the saloon.

Everett Champion strolled over, looking droll. He had both hands plunged deep into trouser pockets when he halted and gazed down his long, thin nose at Perc Whittaker. "Deputy, you got your work cut out for you. I'm withdrawing every complaint I ever made against Logan and am transferring 'em to that bull-necked, ape-built, bushy-bearded wild man instead. Keep him out of my saloon. Never mind the table and chairs. I'll pay for those. You just keep that madman out of my saloon. And as for me closing next Sunday, or any Sunday for that matter ..." Everett shook his grim-featured head from side to side. "Not on your tintype." He turned and strode back over where his barman was setting up drinks as fast as he could fill the glasses, for men crowding to the bar with their loud talk whose backs were turned solidly toward Perc Whittaker.

The only one who made no move to leave his seat was Sam Logan. He sat there, nursing his nickel beer and watching Perc. Even Abner hastened forward to get into the conversation over at the bar.

Perc stood around a while longer, then went outside. Afternoon was marching down the land, leaving its shadowy footprints always on the southeast side of things. Several cowboys were loping into town from the west, raising a banner of dun dust that hung high in the still air like a dirty old shredded blanket. Here and there wisps of smoke stood up from stovepipes where wives and mothers perspired at their Sunday chores of getting the big meal of the day.

Over behind the public corral a little thin drift of smoke stood up from Jonah Reeves's askew stovepipe, too, where Abigail was also doing her Sunday chores.

Perc thought before he braced Jonah again he'd have a little talk with Abigail. For one thing he couldn't outshout Jonah. For another, he wasn't convinced Jonah was a man susceptible to logic or reason. He'd first hear Abigail out and after that, if she didn't have a solution to Jonah's destructive impulses—in the name of the Lord of course—why then Perc, would have to do things his way.

Not that he envisioned the outcome of any tussle they might

have as leaving him virtuously triumphant. Those three range men Jonah had put down were all good men. He knew every one of them, but especially he knew that Snowshoe rider. Still, Jonah's brand of revivalism was unique and it was also somewhat breathtaking, not to mention disruptive, so whether he looked forward to tangling with the bearded old coot or not—there it was. It would have to be done unless Jonah was prepared to listen to reason.

Doc Firth Farraday strolled up, hands in pockets, cocked an eyebrow, and said: "I left the minute the fireworks started in there. A medical man can't run the risk of being made bedfast when he's duty-bound to look after an entire community. And also when he's kind of cowardly to boot. How did it end? Did you corral that bull of the River Styx and lock him up?"

"No," Perc replied, "I didn't. I just warned him."

Doc Farraday pursed his lips and considered a minute speck on his vest for a moment before saying: "Won't work, Perc. He's not the type."

"What won't work? What type isn't he?"

"The kind that'll hitch up and drive on. Or who will listen to reason. I've seen his kind before. Perhaps not as eager to wade in and smite right and left in the service of the Lord, but at least as stubborn and loud."

"I didn't say anything about him having to move on, Doc."

"No," agreed the medical man. "No, sir, you didn't. What I was thinking, Perc, is that all of a sudden Ballester is getting full of disruptive elements. First Sam Logan. Now Jonah Reeves."

Perc gazed thoughtfully at Farraday. That was the truth. First Logan, then Reeves. If people were upset about Logan's hanging around town, what would they now say after the parson's arrival? Moreover, Reeves had played hob at the Golden Slipper. That was the *sanctum sanctorum* for all the menfolk from miles around. If before, in the case of Sam Logan, outside of Johnny West, Ab Fuller, and one or two others, the complaints had been more or less limited, at least outwardly, what would happen now after that sky pilot treed everyone at Everett Champion's place?

"I see what you mean," Perc told Doc Farraday.

The medical man smiled and moved on. He was gray and a little stooped, a former Army doctor, sometimes sweetly pleasant as he'd been just now, and sometimes very acid-tongued. He was about fifty-five but he looked and acted much older. It was rumored he'd contracted malaria during the war in the swamps around Georgia, but no one knew for sure and he rarely spoke of himself.

But one thing was certain. Firth Farraday was a shrewd, observant, highly intelligent man. As far as Perc Whittaker was concerned, he'd just proved it.

CHAPTER FOUR

One time, some years back—in fact, many years back—Perc had known a girl. She'd had golden hair and eyes like Abigail had—cornflower blue—and full red lips that used slowly to smile up at him while she flirted with her eyes. Her name had been Mary and she'd been twelve years old the winter the measles had carried her off.

It was odd the memories a man carried rattling around inside of him. There never could have been much between Perc Whittaker, the grown man, and Mary, the smiling little twelve-year-old girl, but he thought of her every now and then.

He'd known a few women, too, in his time, but he'd never felt much urgency toward them. Probably because he'd never had anything but a range rider's pay to spend on them, which wouldn't have been enough anyway, so when he met Abigail the Tuesday next after Jonah's scene at the Golden Slipper Saloon, he felt a little awkward and uncomfortable. He had his need to talk with her and yet he felt self-conscious about it because he could guess without much divining that she'd probably heard the same words before in other places.

It was early afternoon. She'd borrowed Ab Fuller's stone boat, had one of Jonah's old pelters hitched single to it, and had a water cask roped on the stone boat that she was bucketing full down beside the eastward creek.

It was pleasant down there, except for the myriad flying critters including mosquitoes that acted like they hadn't had a square meal in a year. Willows filtered the heat from the reddening sunlight and a breath of cooling air rose up from the water. She was bending to scoop up a bucket full when he came along and saw her, stopped to watch, and noticed how the sun got tangled in her soft, wavy brown hair and how her skirt drew taut around a solid, muscular thigh. She was something to see. Not very tall but solid and sturdy with her flesh turned golden from the heat and the burn of a July sun.

She heard him, or sensed him, straightened around, and met his glance. He moved over, took the bucket, and upended it into the barrel on the stone boat. "Hot kind of work," he said, avoiding her gaze, turning back to scoop up another bucket load. "Not exactly woman's work, either, ma'am."

She was a little shy with him, at first, but forthright. "Work is medicine, Mister Whittaker. It's the best thing in this world to make sleep come quickly and to keep a person's muscles firm."

He dumped the bucket, peered in to see how nearly full the cask was, and idly said: "Yes'm, but unless a woman's thinking of taking up wrestling or hod hauling, I don't know what she'd need muscles for." He wasn't surprised that she knew his name. Ballester was a small town. It only had one peace officer. He turned and leaned a moment upon the barrel, looking at her. "I've been aiming to talk to you."

"Yes," she murmured, looking him straight in the eye. "I've been expecting you to."

He sighed. That made it a little easier. He turned to scoop up another bucket load. "It's about your pappy."

"Yes, it usually is."

"Well. He sure upset things last Sunday in the saloon."

"Doing the Lord's work, Mister Whittaker."

He emptied the bucket and leaned a moment, watching the water foam and eddy. "There must be more than one Lord, ma'am. Your pappy's Lord seems to talk one way and act another."

"What do you mean?"

"Well, Parson Jonah laid out three cowboys with his fists. At the same time Parson Jonah was roaring about humility and repentance until the windows shook."

"Mister Whittaker, one fights fire with fire, doesn't one?"

Perc leaned upon the barrel, gazing down at her. She stood there half in light, half in shadow, her blouse full and thrusting, her cornflower blue eyes dead level, and her heavy red lips lying closed without pressure. She was a picture of beauty in his sight, and also, more disturbing, of righteousness personified. He stooped to put aside the bucket. Their cask was full.

"There are different kinds of fire, ma'am," he drawled at her. "Even if using his fists was the right way, believe me, Miss Abigail, he's only one man. If he sets a precedent of beating religion into folks, they're just naturally going to beat back, and like I just said, he's only one man."

She half turned to gaze down where the creek was making soft, lapping sounds. Her profile was delicate and fine, putting him in mind of a cameo he'd once seen years ago on a haughty woman in Kansas City. Something about her, aside from her obvious attractions, came over and touched deep down into him. She wasn't very tall, maybe that was it, and except for that old beaver-faced brimstone pappy of hers she seemed alone, or at least lonely. She was sensitive; he could tell that, and she also was not a person who smiled readily, which meant somewhere over the years life had knocked a lot out of her.

He said: "I'm in favor of prayer meetings, Miss Abigail. I've often thought Ballester could even use a church. But folks in cow country just aren't like other people. You can't whang the tar out of them, then turn around and get them to a prayer meeting."

She turned back toward him, looking, he thought, a little wistful. "Mister Whittaker, that man Logan ... what does your town propose to do about him?"

He didn't understand, so he said: "Do? Well, it's pretty much of a free country, ma'am. As long as Logan doesn't get bronco, folks'll leave him alone."

"No, Mister Whittaker. I think you know better than that." She stepped over in the stone boat and looked into the barrel, found it full, and picked up the lid. "Sooner or later they'll run him out of Ballester. We were told how he killed those two Snowshoe riders. We've seen this before in other towns."

"I don't understand what you're getting at, ma'am."

"I'll tell you, Mister Whittaker. We arrived here in the nick of time to save Sam Logan, and to save you people of Ballester from the worst of sins ... judging your fellow men."

He gazed at her, feeling some bitterness and a lot of disappointment. He'd thought, being a handsome woman, she'd have less bigotry and more warmth, be less like old Jonah and more like—well, like he thought a lovely woman ought to be. It was a big let-down for him.

"The judging of Sam Logan is all over," he told her, a slight gruffness coming into his speech. "Anyway, he killed two men. I'd figure you and your pappy'd be dead set against killing, even justifiable killing."

She lifted her eyes to his face. They weren't standing far apart, just the width of the water barrel. He couldn't find a flaw anywhere. "Killing is a part of life, Mister Whittaker. Killing provides us with food, makes it possible for us to survive, keeps our beliefs and our faith triumphant. Nothing that has been ordained is evil ... unless it's used to further the ends of evil."

He thought on that a moment while they stood there, eyeing one another, then he smiled and wagged his head at her. "Like I said before, ma'am, there are different kinds of fire. Frankly I've never before heard a preacher ... or a preacher's daughter, either, for that matter ... preach that killing was justified."

"Each of us interprets the Lord's Word and his works differently, Mister Whittaker," she murmured, meeting his smile with a very vague, very faint twinkle. "Evil isn't simply something black, any more than all virtue is always something white."

"Well, he's sure converted you, ma'am," Perc said, and straightened up off the water barrel.

"Give him a chance to do the same for you, Deputy. Give him a chance in your town."

"I can't. Not if he goes around busting up saloons and whaling the stuffing out of the menfolk. Don't you see, Miss Abigail, folks are beginning to put him in the same category with Sam Logan. This is summertime, to boot. Riders will be coming into town in droves to drink a little and bay at the moon after a hard day's work on the range. They're entitled to that."

"On Sunday, Mister Whittaker?"

He drew in a big breath, and let it out slowly. "Even on Sunday, ma'am. That's the way it's always been. That's probably the way it's going to go right on being."

She reached over to lay a small, brown hand upon his arm. "Mister Whittaker, does doing something over and over again make it right?"

"Well ..." He was thrown off balance by that little hand.

"Of course not. All my father asks is that you let him show them, that's all."

"With his fists, ma'am?"

"No, let me handle that part of it."

"I'll be right glad to. If you can restrain him."

"Let me try. And you ... promise me you'll give him a chance?"

Her earnestness kept him off balance, as well as her closeness. He felt prickles of sweat start under his shirt. He hadn't won this encounter; he knew that. He hadn't even come up with any acceptable compromise

She had. In fact, right from the start, she'd dominated this meeting. He nodded his head while prying his tongue from the roof of his mouth.

"He'll have his chance. But if he goes into the Golden Slipper like he threatened to do next Sunday, Miss Abigail, I'm going to have to lock him up."

She withdrew her hand and stepped back to take up the lines. He saw sunlight strike her wedding band and bounce fiercely off it.

"Thank you, Deputy," she said, clucked at the old horse, and walked away beside Ab Fuller's creaking old stone boat.

He stood there beside the creek for a while, made a cigarette, and smoked it all the way down. He did not believe she'd ever in this world be able to control her father, that old furry-faced cuss had long ago been warped into a particular mold. Fists might beat him down, but, unless Perc Whittaker was far wrong, no words, especially from a slip of a handsome woman, would turn the trick. As Doc Farraday had said, Jonah Reeves was a particular kind of a man—unshakable and probably also unchangeable.

He strolled back up into town and saw Abner Fuller coming out of the jailhouse, angled over to intercept the liveryman in the doorway of his barn, eyed Sam Logan who was sitting there, carving, and followed Abner inside. It was getting late, the light was failing, and over near Abner's harness room a hostler was meticulously filling two coal-oil lamps from a gallon can.

Fuller turned when they were well down the runway and said in a low tone: "Perc, Johnny West was around, looking for you a while back. He asked me to tell you he wanted you to ride out to the ranch as soon as you could."

Perc digested this thoughtfully. West wasted no one's time including his own. "Did he say what was on his mind, Ab?"

"No. But I sort of got an idea it's got to do with that preacher knocking one of his men silly last Sunday."

Perc gazed at the liveryman. "Took him a long time to speak out, if that's it," he said.

Fuller shrugged. "Maybe he's been busy. Running an outfit as big as Snowshoe wouldn't leave a feller a lot of time to ride into town every day or two."

"Maybe you're right," Perc said, and returned to the roadway. Sam Logan was gone from his bench out there. Evening was softly settling, lights glowed, four riders passed up the roadway in a walk, talking back and forth. He couldn't make out their faces or the brands on their horses, but he thought they might be Rainbow men. Abigail Reeves stepped forth from the general store over across the road and moved off.

He watched her. She had a good walk; when an otherwise handsome woman tracked well, it was something to see. Some women sort of quivered when they walked, full of heavy softness. Not Abigail Reeves. He sighed. A good horse walked like that, surer of himself and set solidly in the muscles. It was a hell of a note, comparing a woman like Abigail Reeves to a horse, but he had nothing else to compare her with. Nothing else he knew about, anyway. Besides, it wasn't such a bad comparison. A man who'd come to maturity with horseflesh always around was actually flattering a woman to make such a comparison. But he reflected now, standing in the evening gloom, that probably Miss Abigail wouldn't consider it much of a compliment.

He looked up and down the roadway, then back at Abigail again. She was coming straight across the road toward him, hadn't seen him yet evidently, and was probably headed on through the livery barn to the yonder back alley where the wagon was parked beside the public corral.

He felt uneasiness stir behind his belt buckle. She did that to him, made him feel suddenly less than satisfied with himself, with his lot in life, and in fact with life itself. He wished he hadn't stood there, watching her, because now it was too late to escape.

She looked over and saw him, recognized him, and kept right on walking until she stepped up onto the nearside plank walk and started to move around him into the barn.

"Good evening, Mister Whittaker," she murmured, unsmiling, and passed on by.

"'Evening, ma'am," he replied, keeping his back to her until she'd stepped into the barn, then he slowly turned and looked some more.

"Hell," he growled at himself, straightened back around, and glared across the roadway toward Ev Champion's bar. "Women! What is it about females that makes a man feel like he's got four left feet?"

Abner Fuller stepped through the doorway. "You say something?"

Perc didn't answer Ab. He stepped forth and went hiking on up toward the saloon. Ab called out for him not to forget that Johnny West wanted to see him. He turned and glared at Fuller, then hiked onward again.

Men were beginning to congregate inside the Slipper as usual. Also, as usual, Sam Logan was over there in the shadows on his tilted-back chair nursing his 5¢ glass of beer. There was the customary loud talk and laughter, so two days after it had happened, Parson Reeves's performance had been all but forgotten. At least the men were no longer discussing it, and that was a relief because Perc was sick of discussing it, too.

CHAPTER FIVE

To get to Snowshoe's headquarters ranch was a six-mile ride. Unless a man started early enough, he'd get caught out in the prairie by the burning sun. Perc had, in times past, made this ride too many times as a Snowshoe cowboy to make that mistake. He'd left Ballester an hour before sunrise and arrived at the ranch a half hour after the men had eaten, been detailed to varied chores, and therefore the yard was just about empty when he rode in.

Just about. The man who did the cooking at Snowshoe's headquarters was also the sometime hostler at the barn and corrals. It wasn't customary, but then, as was noted around town, Johnny West ran the Snowshoe thriftily and efficiently. If the *cocinero* finished his cook shack duties and had a little idle time on his hands, he was sent out to drive in fresh horses. And if he didn't like that addition to his ordinary work, he could quit. Most cow-outfit cooks would have quit, too, but sooner or later one came down the pike who needed the work badly enough.

The man saddling up in front of the barn was a wizened, scanty-thatched individual known only as Boots. He'd been the *cocinero* and hostler around Snowshoe for several years now. He knew Percy Whittaker and Perc knew him. Boots was one of those periodic drunks. He might go four months without so much as stepping a foot inside the Golden Slipper. Then he might ride into town in the middle of the day without saying a word to anyone, belly up to Ev Champion's bar, and drink. Drink all that day and maybe all that night. Flop into an empty horse stall over at the livery barn, sleep himself halfway sober, and head straight for the bar and start that steady drinking again. Usually, if folks left him alone, Boots gave no one any trouble. But twice since he'd hit the Ballester country, Perc had jugged him for disorderly conduct—fighting. He hadn't done it because old Boots was likely to hurt anyone. Boots was in his sixties and didn't weigh one hundred and forty pounds with lead in his pockets. It was to keep someone from hurting old Boots that he'd locked him up.

Johnny had once said to Perc that anyone was entitled to let off steam once in a while. This had been after the second arrest when Johnny had taken a day off to drive into town, pour old Boots into the back of the ranch wagon, and solemnly drive back home with him.

Johnny didn't hold it against Boots and Boots didn't hold being jugged against Perc Whittaker. It was a loosely understood agreement between all of them, so when Boots saw who the visitor was who'd come riding in from the direction of town, he left off rigging out his horse and said: "Wait here, Deputy. Johnny's in the cook shack, havin' a cup of java. I'll fetch him."

Perc swung down, watered his horse at the trough, and gazed around the empty, dusty ranch yard. A door slammed across the way, and Johnny and Boots came walking over. Perc looped his reins so the horse could sip at his leisure and waited. There was a little thin shade in front of the barn.

"Tried to find you in town yesterday," said West, on coming up.

"So Ab told me. I can guess what it's about." Perc thumbed back his hat. Sometimes it got tiresome making excuses, but it was part of his job, the biggest part, it seemed. "If it's about that rider of yours getting knocked out in the Slipper day before yesterday, Johnny, I've got a sort of promise it won't happen again. That preacher just took everyone by surprise, me included."

West lowered himself to the edge of the water trough and looked wryly up at Perc. "Tell him, Boots," he said quietly. The *cocinero* came close in a crabbed little walk and screwed up his face at the taller deputy sheriff. "You ever heard of a feller named John Reed?" he asked in his piping voice.

Perc nodded. He'd heard plenty about a man named John Reed. Stage robbery, bank robbery, payroll robbery, ten years in Fort McHenry for making off with an Army quartermaster's payroll—wagon and all. Five years in …

"Well you got him in your town, Deputy. Jonah Reeves he calls himself now. But I don't forget faces and all that beaver hair don't change a blamed thing. He's got a scar from below his ear down across his cheek into them whiskers. I was there the day he got that, Deputy. He tried to break away from a cavalry escort taking him to Fort McHenry. I was on the horse next to the captain that run him down and swung that saber that laid his face open. I'd know that feller anywhere on this lousy earth. He's calling himself Parson Reeves now, but that's not his real name. He's John Reed, the outlaw!"

Johnny West kept looking up at Perc. Old Boots hitched himself along into the shade and also stared. Perc reached up, lifted his hat to let a little cool air pass across his sweat-matted hair, then slowly re-settled the hat upon his head. He was trying to recall the last thing he'd heard or read about John Reed, the notorious highwayman. He thought it had been a small item in a newspaper about Reed being released from prison a couple of years back.

"Well," said Johnny West, near to grinning at Perc's long expression.

"Well what?" Perc asked.

"What you figure to do about him?"

"Find out first whether he's still wanted or not, I guess."

"That's logical," Johnny opined, and stood up off the edge of the trough. "But if he's not wanted … what then? Listen, Perc, first it was that Sam Logan, now it's old John Reed. You've been too easy in town. Folks aren't going to like it when they find out who else is making Ballester their headquarters. They're going to start saying you're shielding men who've got no …"

"Shielding? I'm not shielding anyone," growled Perc, irritated. "If Reed's served his time, then that's the end of it."

"Maybe," agreed West pleasantly. "But Perc, old dogs don't learn new tricks. John Reed's notorious in a dozen states and territories. He wasn't a young man when they threw him into prison the last time. Ever since Boots recognized him last Sunday in Ev's saloon, I've been thinking. Why would a man like Reed grow a big bushy beard and get himself up as a preacher, which would be the best disguise in the world for a man like him, unless he had something in mind like maybe blowing safes or something like that?"

"What safes?" Perc asked, still irritated. "Ev's got a safe and there's one at the general store. There's never more than a couple hundred dollars in either one of them."

"Sure. Maybe that's right, Perc. But Reed wouldn't know that."

Boots took his boss' side by saying in his piping voice: "Deputy, I've been doin' a little calculatin', too, and I come up with something else. Why don't Logan push on? He knows by now no one's goin' to hire him on. I'll tell you … because him and John Reed are in this together, that's why."

"In what together?" snarled Perc, turning on the cook.

Boots snapped his lips closed in the face of Perc's anger and looked pleadingly at Johnny West for support. He got it. West looked Whittaker straight in the eye and said: "No one who is that fast with a gun is a commonplace rider, Perc. Logan's a killer, an experienced gunfighter. Even without that mother-of-pearl on his gun he'd still be recognizable as a gunfighter. What's the matter

with you anyway? Does he have to wipe out half the town before
you start using your head?"

Perc's irritability turned to solid disgust. Not with Boots and
Johnny West particularly, but more with himself. It perhaps wasn't
his fault he hadn't seen Jonah Reeves as anything other than one
of those fire-and-brimstone old itinerant ministers, but what West
had just said about Sam Logan was undeniably true. Logan was too
good with a gun to be a common, everyday cowboy. He turned,
released his horse's reins, hauled the beast over, and stepped up
across him.

"What're you going to do?" Johnny West inquired, looking
up. "Wait until this evening, Perc, and I'll fetch in my crew. No
point in getting yourself killed just because you made a mistake. We
understand. Besides, it could've happened to anyone."

"You stay out of town tonight," Perc said, giving West a hard
glance. "If there's one thing I don't need it's a bunch of Snowshoe
men hooting and rooting through town."

He rode out of the yard with the sun holding to one high
position in the faded July sky as though it, too, were now his enemy.
It burned down across his shoulders and back until just before he
got into sight of town again, then it reluctantly began to sink lower
down the smoky heavens.

Made a mistake! When he'd worked for West as a rider, he'd had
a lot of respect for his cow savvy. It seemed that having cow savvy
didn't necessarily ensure that a man had any other kind of savvy. In
fact, he told himself a trifle resentfully, maybe that ensured that he
didn't have any other kind.

He hadn't made any mistake. Sure, Sam Logan was deadly with a
gun, faster and more accurate than ordinary range riders were. Maybe
he even was a gunfighter like Johnny had said. But he *hadn't* killed
Banning and Johnson as a gunfighter; he did those two killings in
self-defense. If Johnny wanted to think otherwise, that was his priv-
ilege—but two inquests had proved Logan had been justified.

As for Jonah—or John Reed, rather—that was something else again. But it irritated him that old Boots had recognized Reed and had gone to West instead of to him. Now, West was feeling full of righteousness and condescension, and that made Percy feel irritable all over again, made him feel as though he wasn't capable of doing his job and West knew it, which wasn't true.

He got into town with dusk settling, swung down.

Ab Fuller stepped forth to take the reins and said: "Well, was I right about what he wanted?"

Perc glared and said: "Go to hell, will you."

He went across to the café, ate a big meal, shunned the easy conversation that filled the place, and afterward walked over to his office at the jailhouse to take down his musty stacks of posters and go through them until he found a good picture of John Reed—without the beard and with his hair cut. Reed had been much younger when that picture had been taken but the eyes were the same, unflinching, tough, fierce, and piercing eyes.

He folded that poster and pocketed it, made a smoke, and went outside to stand a while in the coolness of early evening while he tried hard to recall what it was he'd read about John Reed a year or two back.

Ballester had no telegraph office. Its only constant link with the outside world was the stage line. He decided to write a letter to the sheriff over at the county seat in the morning, requesting all the up-to-date news on Reed, and send it along in the personal care of the stage driver.

He killed the smoke and went hiking northward up as far as Ab's barn. There, he cut inside and went all the way through out into the back alley. The Reeves wagon was barely visible where a slit of orange lamplight glowed past the back door, up beside the community corral. He started in that direction. He'd been willing to let things slide before, after his earlier talk with Abigail, but not now. Now things were different and whatever was to be done he'd do his own way.

"Hey, Percy," someone said softly, and stepped out of the alleyway shadows toward him. "It's Doc."

He waited until he recognized Farraday, then gravely nodded. "You lose something back here?" he inquired.

Farraday smiled and shook his head. "Just coming back from a house call. A case of whooping cough."

"Oh."

They stood eyeing each other for a while before Farraday said, making his voice soft and his words very slow: "I heard a rumor today about your friend Logan, Percy."

"My friend, hell," snarled Perc.

Farraday's eyebrows shot up. "Excuse me," he murmured. "I didn't know that was a sore subject. I didn't mean anything, just a phrase."

"What did you hear about him?"

"There were some men passing through on their way up north. They stopped at the Slipper for a cool drink and saw him there. They told Ev Champion that he was some kind of a gunman."

"What does that mean," growled Perc, annoyed all over again. "How is a man some kind of a gunman? He's either a gunman, or he's not."

"Percy," said Doc Farraday, beginning to stiffen a little toward the deputy. "All I'm doing is passing something along I heard today in the belief that it may be of some use to you. That's all." Farraday paused, then said: "One thing is obvious to me, too, and it should be just as obvious to you. Sam Logan's hanging around Ballester can't bring any good and it might bring more bad. More killings. Good night."

Farraday walked on and Perc twisted to gaze after him briefly, then he straightened around, considered the light coming from the Reeves wagon, lifted his shoulders high, dropped them, and turned off to the right, heading over toward the empty plot of ground between the corrals and Fuller's barn where he could cross on through and emerge upon the main roadway. Over in that direction the lights—and sounds—of the Golden Slipper were noticeable. He'd have a talk with Everett Champion first, then he'd have a talk with Sam Logan. Finally he'd go have a talk with Jonah Reeves or whatever his name was.

The irritability lessened in him but did not entirely atrophy. Again, though, he was annoyed with himself. He should have braced Logan long ago, should have run him out of town as everyone had urged him to. Now when he did it, the heads would nod and the gossip would start. He could almost hear it. *Took Whittaker long enough. He sure isn't very smart, letting two like that settle in our town. Well, what can you expect from an ex-cowboy who's never had any real lawman training?*

He stepped up onto the far plank walk and strode past some idling range riders by the Slipper's hitch rack without even looking at them. The cowboys fell silent, raised their eyebrows at one another, turned, and swiftly moved to follow Perc inside. From the look on the deputy's face, it seemed like there might be fireworks.

CHAPTER SIX

Everett Champion took Perc down to the far end of the bar and said there had been a couple of floaters in earlier and they had told him they'd known Sam Logan down in Arizona. Champion couldn't recall the name of the town exactly and Perc said that didn't matter. What he specifically wanted to know was what those drifters had said about Logan.

"They said," confided Everett, dropping his voice until Perc had to lean over to hear him at all, "Logan had quite a reputation as a gunfighter in Arizona and over in New Mexico."

"That's all they said?"

Champion nodded. "What more'd they have to say, Perc? He's already killed two men in Ballester."

"And been cleared by a court, Everett," growled Perc, straightening up off the bar. "I'm going to have a talk with him."

Champion moved quickly and caught Perc's sleeve. "Don't you mention me in this at all," he begged. "I never said anything against him ... especially."

Perc pulled free. "Quit worrying," he insisted, and walked away.

Where Logan had staked his claim over against the dingy northward wall, a man commanded not only a perfect view of the saloon's full length but he also could see anyone entering the place before they could see him. Just coincidence, Perc told himself, and grimaced. It was the same kind of coincidence when a lion is found lying on an outstretched oak limb above a deer run.

He took a chair and spun it, dropped down next to Logan, and exchanged a civil little nod with the shorter, older man. The room was noisy and smoky, men moved restlessly along the bar and out among the card tables. Riders were still coming in from the ranches and an occasional townsman passed them at the door homeward bound. It was, all in all, a pleasantly masculine scene and Sam Logan, tilted back in his chair, seemed to be enjoying it even though no one spoke to him and only a few men nodded as they moved past him.

Perc watched the noisy confusion for a moment, then said: "Sam, when're you going to give up?"

Logan turned and carefully studied Perc's features. He understood at once and said: "Pretty soon, Deputy, pretty soon. It's a good little town and the range is rich, but living on four bits a day and being down to your last eleven dollars skunks a man. I'd sort of figured maybe they'd look at things the way they really happened and someone'd take a chance and hire me. They aren't going to, though, are they?"

"It doesn't look like it. I've been waiting for that, too."

"The townsmen seem to be getting edgy about me hurting business."

"Something like that, Sam."

"And you? What's your stand, Deputy?"

"You've figured that out, Sam. If I'd been contrary, I'd have talked to you long before."

Logan nodded, sipped from his carefully hoarded nickel glass of beer, and looked solemn. "Care for a drink?" he eventually asked. When Perc shook his head, Logan said: "Tell 'em to rest easy, Deputy. I'll be pulling out pretty quick now." He looked down into his glass, considered the last big mouthful of brew, threw back his head, and drained it off and afterward smacked his lips. "There were a couple of boys in here today who looked familiar to me. They talked to Champion … isn't that it?"

Perc side-stepped a direct answer, saying only: "If they looked familiar to you, it's possible you looked the same way to them. This time of year a fellow can meet old friends any time, Sam, any place."

Logan softly shook his head. "They weren't old friends, Deputy. They were a couple of tinhorn renegades from down south, card cheats, back-shooters, two-bit horse thieves."

Perc's attention turned sharp. "Outlaws?" he said. "You recognized them as wanted men?"

Logan didn't answer right away. He eased his chair down off the wall, leaned to place his empty beer glass upon a vacant nearby table, and stood up. "I couldn't swear about how bad they're wanted, Deputy. All I know is that I've seen 'em before down south, and the word was they were real undesirables. What else did they tell Champion? That I was a bad one?"

"Something like that, Sam."

Logan stood in thought, and Perc gazed up at him from his seated position. Sam Logan was a hard man to figure, he didn't look mean or treacherous. He even had little smiling wrinkles up around his shrewd blue eyes, and yet there was that mother-of-pearl .45 on his hip to remind Perc and everyone else how lethal he was with guns.

Logan raised his eyes, settled them upon Perc, and gravely nodded. "See you around, Deputy," he said, turned and started on across the room. Perc watched him reach the roadside doors and shoulder through, out into the night. He let off a quiet sigh and also arose. That much was done; Logan would be moving on soon, which was all he'd wished to make sure of. Now he'd go have that talk with old Jonah Reeves—or John Reed, or whatever his cussed name was. As he started forward, Everett came around the bar and cut in front of him. Old Ev's sly, wrinkled-up, prune-like features were sharply inquisitive.

"You didn't tell him, did you?" he asked.

Perc said: "I didn't have to, Ev, he already knew. Seems he recognized those two boys from Arizona at the same time they recognized him."

"Well, but if you mentioned me, he'd liable to …"

"He said for you and the others around town not to worry. He also said he's pulling out in a few days."

Champion's face relaxed, losing its inquisitive sharpness. "Fine, Perc. That's just fine. Now, go get rid of that other misfit and things'll be right back to normal, won't they?"

Perc didn't answer and walked on out of the place. It was a pleasant warm night with a weak moon and a high rash of brilliant stars scattered like diamond dust across a purple tapestry. There were little groups of men standing here and there along the walkways, smoking and casually gossiping. All in all it was a very peaceful scene. He could see the lamplight coming from the rear of Jonah's wagon over yonder behind the public corral. It reassured him because he hadn't been certain the old cuss and his daughter didn't retire early. There surely wasn't much in Ballester to appeal to those two after sundown. He stepped down and started across the wide roadway. It must be hard on a woman like Abigail, he mused, being cooped up in a wagon with an old fanatic like Jonah. Whether he was a preacher or an outlaw, one thing was sure—he was narrowly set in his ways, and right or wrong they'd get almighty boring to a girl after a few months. Besides, she was too handsome to be cooped up like that all the time. She was the kind of a woman who'd like beauty and music and moonlight walks on balmy summer nights.

He was almost through the vacant lot beside Ab's barn before his thoughts came back down to the prosaic business at hand. What brought them down so suddenly was a blurry shadow over near the wagon. He halted, watched it a moment, decided it was Abigail because it was shorter than a man would ordinarily be, and when it faded out in the layers of gloom, he moved on again. He didn't try to intercept her, but went instead to the rear of the rig and knocked lightly on the door.

When the panel opened, he was looking straight up into Abigail's face. He blinked at her, stepped back, and threw a look up where that blurry shadow had been. Of course it was no longer visible.

"Can I help you, Deputy?" she called softly to him.

He stepped back again and removed his hat. "If your pappy's not asleep, I'd like a word with him, ma'am."

She started to step aside for Perc to enter the wagon. Behind her loomed up the massively bear-like silhouette of her father. He was holding aloft a little reading lamp. "Who is it?" he rumbled, and when Abigail said it was Mister Whittaker, the deputy sheriff, Jonah shouldered around her and overflowed past the opened door holding down his lamp to see Perc's face. "Ahhh," he mumbled, handed Abigail the lamp, and came on through the door, down the little set of steps into the night, and closed the door behind him. "Good evening, Deputy," he rumbled. "What can I do for you?"

"Take a little walk with me," said Perc, conscious of Abigail on the other side of that door.

"Be right happy to. Where'll we walk?"

"Just down the alley a piece, Parson."

They strolled along, one of them tall and solidly made, the other one shorter, nearly twice as broad, and sort of rolling as he moved along. They got down near the back alley exit of Ab Fuller's barn and Perc stopped. It was gloomy out here but it was also deserted.

Perc turned, met the piercing eyes of the older, bearded man, and said quietly: "John Reed."

Parson Reeves stared and said nothing for a long time. He eventually twisted to peer back up toward the wagon, seemed satisfied they were far enough from it, then looked elsewhere around the alley and seemed satisfied about that, too. "I appreciate your thoughtfulness," he rumbled in a low, grave tone of voice. "I sort of had you pegged as a considerate man, Deputy. All right, I'm John Reed."

"Why this get-up as a parson, Mister Reed?" asked Perc.

"It's no get-up, Deputy. I saw the error of my ways in prison. That was after Abigail's husband died in a dirty little Mex town in a gunfight leaving my girl alone. I took to the Bible trail. That's all there is to it. There are hundreds of young men in the West who need someone like me, not just any kind of a preacher, but my kind. When I was a young feller, I ran into a lot of those ministers with their cussed collars on backward and they didn't know what they were talking about … mentioning evil and evil-doers. But, Deputy, *I know*. I've been through it all. I know what I'm talking about."

"I see," murmured Perc, watching the older man and wondering if he was that good of an actor.

"Maybe you do," went on John Reed. "But I sort of doubt it, son. I spent the first forty years of my life steeped in iniquity. I figure to spend what's left to me making amends, and if I can prevent just one wild young buckaroo from riding the same downward trail I took, I'll have done my duty as His servant. Just one man, Deputy."

"About Miss Abigail's husband, Parson …?" said Perc, deliberately letting his voice trail off.

"I stood up for them," rumbled the older man, dropping his eyes. "Married my own daughter to a bank robber and worse. It sticks in my throat, Deputy. But like I told you, I was a man sunk deep in iniquity. Then he robbed a Wells, Fargo safe and had to run for it. I was in prison when she wrote me he'd been killed in some filthy dive down in Mexico and she was working at a laundry down near Tempe in Arizona. That clinched it for me, my own little motherless girl left alone to sweat out her life at labor because of me and my evilness."

Perc heard the gruffness creep into that rumbling bass voice and felt mean for having pushed Reed into this baring of his soul. And yet he had another unpleasant task still to perform. "Parson, it'll only be a matter of time before everyone hereabouts finds out who you are. I doubt like the devil that you'll ever be able to preach a sermon in this town or take up an offering."

"Yes. What you're saying, Deputy, is that you figure it'd be better all around if I hitched up and drove on."

"Yes," murmured Perc, feeling even meaner.

"Well. Thanks for being civil, Deputy. Since I've been on the Bible trail not many lawmen've been as decent as you have." Reed lifted his head. "And I know about how your thoughts are running because I've come onto this same thing before. You're wondering if old John Reed isn't as big a fraud now as a parson as he was a hell-roaring outlaw."

Perc didn't deny that but neither did he confirm it. All he said was: "A local range man recognized you in the saloon last Sunday. He figured you were up to something here in Ballester."

"Sure he did, Deputy, and who can blame him? I made my bed of thorns and I don't deny I ought to have to lie in it. That's part of my punishment." Reed raised his mighty arms and tilted back his head, his beard stood out, and coldly impersonal starlight shone down across his battered old face. "But for how long, oh, Lord," he groaned. "For how long?"

Perc shifted his stance and looked swiftly around. He felt embarrassed. The alleyway was empty.

Reed dropped his arms and lowered his head. He studied Whittaker's face a long time, then inclined his head. "I'll do as you say. We'll hitch up in a few days and move on. But I hate to do it, Deputy, because, believe me, there's a heap more iniquity in this town than you know … than you got any idea about." He paused and a faint, crafty light shone in his pale stare. "I'll leave next Monday or Tuesday. Will that be all right?"

Perc shifted his feet again. The old cuss was going to hang around until next Sunday. He turned this over in his mind and doggedly said: "Mister Reed, no more saloon-chousing come Sunday. I told Miss Abigail I'd lock you up if you did that again."

"Aye. She told me, Deputy. She told me of you helping fill the water barrel at the creek. You made a decent impression on her and she's a girl that's got reason to be skeptical of men."

"Well, I meant it, Mister Reed. I sure don't want you to think I'm throwing my weight around behind this badge because that's not it at all. But Ballester's been a peaceful, orderly place up until recently, and I'd like for it to be that way again, so … you stay out of Ev Champion's place. All right?"

"All right, Deputy. But it goes against the grain. Saloons and the Sabbath don't mix."

"Nevertheless …"

"You have my word, Deputy," Reed rumbled, and held out a hand as thick and broad as a bear's paw. "I'm beholden to you, too. John Reed never forgets a favor."

They shook, and the older man turned and shuffled back up toward his wagon. Perc stood a while, watching and feeling both hopeful and skeptical, then he fell to wondering about that elusive blurry shadow he'd seen earlier skulking around the wagon. Of one thing he was certain—that hadn't been Abigail.

CHAPTER SEVEN

It was getting late so he walked down to the jailhouse to lock the door before heading on over to the boarding house. He had no prisoners—hadn't had in fact for over a month now—but he did have a wall rack of rifles and shotguns in there not to mention some files and other things, so he made a habit of locking up every night before heading for home.

It was dark under the warped wooden awning that shaded the front of the jailhouse. He hooked the big padlock and turned to cast a look up and down the roadway. There weren't many lights still glowing—up at the Slipper of course brightness still glowed, and across the road on the same side as the jailhouse, at Fuller's livery barn there was more light, but otherwise, except for a rare soft glow here and there, the town was dark.

Usually he made a circuit of the tie racks. Sometimes careless or callous men left horses hitched at the racks all night. When that happened, he hunted up the owners, routed them out, and made them go down and take their animals over to the livery barn. But tonight the only critters standing patiently at the racks were up in front of Ev's bar and cowboys never forgot their mounts, so they could go on home.

But he didn't. For some reason he did not clearly understand he stood down there in front of the jailhouse and made a cigarette, lit it, and stood with the thing drooping from his lips. He had an odd feeling, a sort of uneasy sensation. He'd first developed it when talking with Sam Logan. It was as though, as John Reed had quietly said, there was something going on around Ballester he didn't know about.

He went back over both those conversations word for word to the best of his recollection, and all this did was strengthen that feeling. It was a little like waiting for a hidden bomb to detonate.

"Nerves," he muttered aloud. "It's been a long day, a long ride out to Snowshoe and back. Just nerves."

He removed the cigarette and gazed at its sullenly red little glowing tip. Something passing through darkness off on his right made a faint, sharp impression on his senses. He went right on eyeing the smoke, waiting for that little wispy movement to be repeated, drawing himself up very carefully for swift movement.

"Mister Whittaker …?"

He turned, recognizing the huskiness of the voice even before he sighted her face and figure through the gloom. She had her hair swept severely back and parted at the center. Her dress was of some dark and rusty material that fitted close up above, pinched in flat to the waist, then flared. It blended perfectly with the night.

"Yes'm," he said, dropping the smoke and grinding it out to gain a moment's respite from the near start he'd had.

"I wanted to talk to you. I'm sorry if I startled you."

He raised his head. She was closer now and gazing straight up at him. He made a small, crooked smile at her. "You've got good eyesight if you can see that well in the dark, Miss Abigail." He began turning back toward the jailhouse door. "We can talk inside, if you wish."

"No, please … can't we just walk southward to the edge of town?"

"Sure, ma'am," he said, and turned to move off at her side. For a while she said no more. He was conscious of the soft rustle of her skirt. He was also conscious of her closeness and of the fragrance of her hair. Where she finally paused, it was far enough southward so that only a very faint echo of the sounds coming from Champion's saloon were audible. There were a few residences down here, all dark and quiet now.

"Mister Whittaker ... my father told me."

He stood waiting and watching. He could have guessed old John Reed would have confided in her. He even wished a trifle wistfully he might also confide in her.

"At the creek, Mister Whittaker, you said you'd give him a chance if I promised you he wouldn't fight any more." She half turned and lifted her eyes. "Aren't you going to keep your word?"

"Miss Abigail, things happen. Things change. I'm not going back on my word, though. He doesn't have to pull out until next week. In fact, ma'am, I didn't tell him he had to go ... *he* told me."

"But you meant that we had to. It's the same thing." She drew in a big breath. "Mister Whittaker, he's been getting run out of towns for several years now. He's not a young man and what he wants more than anything else is just to settle somewhere. To stop moving. To preach his sermons and have a small house somewhere and ... do *good* things."

Perc looked back up the roadway where the orange squares of light lay low in roadway dust. He looked down again. "It's not me, ma'am, it's the town."

"It's always the town, Mister Whittaker, it's never the law or the lawmen," she replied a little ruefully.

"Well, I'm only a deputy sheriff. I've told folks he was harmless. Then today I found out who he really is, and that's what changed things."

"Yes, of course it has. You can't trust John Reed."

"No ma'am. Not I. Maybe *I* could trust him. I could sure trust *you* and if you said he wasn't the same John Reed, that'd be plenty good for me. But not for the town. They'll find out who he really is within a day or two, then it wouldn't matter how he's reformed, they'd only recall all the other stuff about him."

She turned and paced along again. He hesitated a moment before trudging along after her. They were near the southernmost end of town now, beyond the homes and down among some dilapidated abandoned old shacks. He reached forth to halt her where the plank walk ended, brought her around, and said: "Abigail, one thing I don't believe is that he just happened to hit on Ballester as the place to put down his roots. I can't exactly explain that, but last Sunday he said some things at the Golden Slipper that gave the first inkling it wasn't just coincidence he came to my town. Again tonight, when we talked in the alleyway, there was something behind his words again."

"And so you've deduced that he's here to blow a safe or rob your bank."

"Ma'am, we don't have a bank and the only two safes in town never have any money in them."

"Then what is it, Mister Whittaker?"

"I don't know, and that's what's got me wondering."

They stood for a long moment, gazing at one another. She finally turned her back to him and stood quietly looking far down the star-washed night. The range southward ran on endlessly toward some far-away mountains, invisible now because of the weak moonlight. The air was redolent of the acrid odors of lupine and chaparral and buckbrush. It was a strong scent but a good one.

"He could do good for your town," she murmured finally. "He probably told you that all he wants is to keep men from making the same mistakes he made when he was younger."

"He also told me about your husband, and I'm sorry about that."

She faced around. "There's no need for you to be. The day we were married he left and I never saw him again. Mister Whittaker … I never loved him. He was my father's riding pardner, that's all."

Perc cleared his throat and rummaged for something to say. "Well, I reckon we've got a few scars, ma'am. I'm sorry about you folks leaving. I guess I'm sort of selfishly sorry."

Her liquid soft eyes widened a little. "Selfishly sorry?" she murmured. "I don't understand."

"It's nothing, ma'am. Now I reckon we'd better be hiking on back. He'll miss you and get to worrying. It's getting late."

She started strolling back with him, her head bowed, her thoughts evidently running on ahead of them. Finally she said: "Deputy, did you also suggest that Sam Logan move on?"

He was mildly surprised at that and said: "No, not exactly. It worked out about the same way with Logan. *He* told me. I didn't have to tell him."

She said no more until they were passing the jailhouse and a pair of horsemen loped past out in the roadway, southward bound, their free and easy banter musical in the otherwise gloomy hush. "I suppose you've figured out that Mister Logan has his load to carry, too, Deputy."

He looked closely at her. "Like I said down yonder, we all have some scars."

"Yes, but a man like you, Mister Whittaker, doesn't really know what scars people can acquire in this life."

He stopped and said: "Miss Abigail, my paw was a drunk and disappeared. My mother got carried off in an epidemic on the Kansas plains. I've been cutting my own trail since I was twelve. It's been a long haul from there to here."

She seemed a trifle confused by his sudden intensity. Before, he'd sounded quietly confident and quite unemotional. "I'm sorry," she whispered without raising her face. "I was carried away, Mister Whittaker." She swept his face with an upward tilt of her eyes and made an ironic little smile with her heavy mouth. "It was self-pity, I guess. I'm sorry. I don't really blame you. Not really. And we'll go on like my father said."

"I wish you didn't have to!" he exclaimed in the same disturbed, sharply intense tone of voice. "What I meant back there about being selfishly sorry ... I meant you." He paused, breathed deeply, collected his thoughts, and said: "I meant, if you weren't leaving, I'd feel a whole lot better."

Now her expression turned smooth and impassive toward him. For a fraction of a second something dark and turgid stirred in the depths of her eyes, then it was gone and she said softly—"Good night, Mister Whittaker."—turned and walked slowly away from him.

He stood without moving for a long time even after she was no longer visible, then he said a terse swear word at himself. But at once his candid defenses rallied, he'd meant what he'd revealed to her. If he'd handled the matter clumsily, that was his fault, but otherwise he'd been honest.

Still, the whole thing was confused and confusing. He stepped down off the plank walk and started shuffling across through roadway dust toward the opposite side of the road on his way home.

A man could be mature and seasoned, even hardened, in all the little intricacies of everyday existence—everyday survival—and still, at thirty years of age, feel like the sand was being sucked from underneath him when he came against a woman who drew him like a magnet.

He could be hard as iron and as tough as whang leather. He could read men like a book and weather patterns as easily as his own palm. He could tell a horse's disposition from one good look into the crit-ter's eye, and still be as helpless as a gummer cub bear in something like this other thing. There was a light on at the boarding house. He scarcely saw it as he turned in at the gate and clumped on up the boardwalk toward the porch. There was a man sitting, slouched and easy, on the porch swing, too, but until Perc was reaching for the first step with an extended foot, he didn't see him, either.

It was Doc Farraday smoking a long cheroot and pensively

studying the clear-purple heavens. He stirred, the swing squeaked, and Perc stopped stonestill for as long as it took to run a searching look on ahead.

"Been waiting for you," said the medical man, removing his cheroot. "It's a pleasant night and this is a quiet spot. You know, Deputy, a man's greatest pleasures come from things that don't cost him a dime. Look at that sky."

Perc moved on up, gazed at Farraday's thin, ascetic profile, read the expression correctly, and reached for a chair.

"And maybe his greatest disappointments come from the same things, Doc," he muttered. "What's on your mind?"

Farraday straightened up, drew in his thin, long legs and removed his cigar. His eyes, grave and hooded behind the half droop of lids, shone with a shrewd, hard glitter. "In my line of work, Deputy, after you've been at it a number of years, you develop a sixth sense about people. This evening a man came to me with a suppurating bullet wound in his right arm. Now my sixth sense told me he was not the kind of man I'd enjoy meeting on a dark night if I had a money belt full of greenbacks on me."

"Stranger?"

Farraday nodded. "And I'd say from the looks of him and his exhausted condition, he'd been traveling a long time."

"What was his name, where'd he say he came from?"

"My friend, his kind say nothing. He took off his coat and hat and tossed down a ten-dollar bill, ripped off a filthy bandage, and glared at me. Once, when I was cleaning the wound, he swore. That was the total extent of our conversation." Doc Farraday leaned back and gazed sardonically over at Perc. "I can tell you one thing, I've seen hundreds of wounds just like that one in my time. That man was moving *away* from whoever shot him at the time he stopped that bullet."

Perc waited but Farraday was finished. He took a long pull off his cheroot and let the smoke trickle up past his deep-set, hooded eyes.

"Is he still in town?" Perc inquired, and got a shrug for an answer.

"I saw him to the door. There were two horses at my rack out front and another man was out there, sitting on one of them." Farraday paused, gazed at the end of his stogie, and said thoughtfully: "I'd hazard a guess they didn't go far. The man I worked on was gray around the mouth from sheer exhaustion. Even if he'd wanted to, he couldn't have ridden another ten miles without collapsing. And one last thing, Deputy, that bullet wound was acquired at least a week back. Possibly two weeks back."

"How bad was it?"

"Well, there was no blood poisoning, although I don't know why. The man had wrapped a filthy handkerchief around it. But I'd say he'll be at least two months recovering whereas, if he'd stopped somewhere for competent treatment, it wouldn't have troubled him for perhaps three weeks or a month."

Farraday stood up. Perc got up with him. That uneasy feeling was becoming stronger in Perc again. When Farraday said —"Good night."—and walked down off the porch, Perc answered mechanically without actually being aware of answering at all.

CHAPTER EIGHT

In a town no larger than Ballester that had very little transient trade it would have been impossible for a pair of strangers such as Doc Farraday had described to go unnoticed. Particularly if one of them was ill from a festering arm wound. But Perc found no one aside from Farraday who'd seen any such men. He even made a personal inspection of Fuller's barn, seeking ridden-down horses, and the stores around town for some sign of strangers buying supplies.

He had no idea who the illusive strangers were but he was curious about the one who had been shot from behind. Men were either ambushed from behind, or else they were fleeing from someone when they were winged like that. His private guess was that these two had been fleeing, had probably committed some lawless act somewhere south of Ballester, and one of them had stopped lead in the course of a wild flight.

He rode up the stage road out of town, looking for tracks that might branch off somewhere, perhaps leading toward one of the many arroyos over the range. He found plenty of such tracks, but they all turned out to belong to range riders who were heading for Snowshoe or Rainbow range. He knew most of the places where an injured man could hide out for a while. He scouted water holes and grassy glades and turned up nothing, not even any signs where two riders had paused a while to rest their jaded mounts.

He spent the entire day like that, rode back into town late in the evening, tired, hungry, and thirsty, left his horse with Ab, and went across to the café. Afterward he strolled on up and had a little conversation with Everett Champion. But the only strangers Ev remembered were those two floaters who had drifted through a day earlier and who had recognized Sam Logan.

Then Perc made a discovery. After almost two months of punctually perching either in front of Fuller's barn or up at Champion's saloon, Sam Logan was gone. There was no trace of Logan at all. Fuller didn't even know when Sam had removed his horse from the public corral.

Perc went over among the shacks beyond town, located the one he'd thought Logan had been sleeping in, found where someone had flung down his bedroll, where he'd smoked and scuffed the earthen floor removing his boots, but found nothing else, no boots, no bedroll, no Sam Logan.

He went back to his office at the jailhouse, shuffled through the mail that had come since his departure from town earlier, found nothing interesting, remembered that he'd meant to write the sheriff, and shrugged that off as now being unimportant. He then went along to Doc Farraday's place and asked the medical practitioner to accompany him back to his office.

There, he put Farraday down at his desk, set a pile of dusty old Wanted posters in front of him, and said: "Find him, Doc. If he's not in there, I'm stumped. I'll be over talking to Ab Fuller, but I'll be back before you get through that stack."

Farraday cocked an eyebrow at the pile, then went to work. Perc went up the road as far as the livery barn and found Ab leaning unconcernedly in his doorway shade, mopping his neck and face. "Summer's finally here," grumbled Fuller. "Even the dog-goned sun doesn't have wits enough to go down until nine o'clock."

"Ab, there were a couple of strangers in town last night. I went through your barn early this morning looking for tucked-up, strange horses. You weren't around. I didn't find anything, but I thought you might have seen a couple of men like that during the day."

Fuller furrowed his brow in thought and was totally quiet for a while, then he ruefully shook his head. "I'm sure sorry," he muttered. "Actually, though, it's been so blessed hot today I've been sort of keeping back in the shade. There could've been such a pair ... only I sure never saw 'em." Fuller's hangdog expression brightened. "Have you seen Ev? Maybe he saw these fellers you're looking for if you left early this morning."

"Yeah," Perc said wearily. "I'll talk to him later." He turned and went slowly back through the evening heat to his jailhouse. Just before he reached the building, a lounging man straightened up off the front of another building and stepped forth with a slow, amiable smile. The man was unknown to Perc; he was clearly a range rider from his appearance and his dress.

"'Evenin'," he said in a drawling voice. "I been sort of keepin' an eye peeled for you, Deputy. I wanted to ask you a question. Me 'n' a friend of mine come into town yesterday and stopped off for a cool beer at the saloon up yonder. We seen a fellow sittin' up there with a pearl-handled gun. His name's Sam Logan. What I wanted to know ... did you know who he was?"

Perc placed this stranger right away from his statement. He'd be one of the two men who'd recognized Logan the day before and who'd warned Everett Champion about Logan.

Eyeing this man closely and remembering also what Logan had said about this man and his pardner, Perc said: "Well, I can't rightly say I know too much about Logan. He's had two gunfights in Ballester."

"Yeah," grunted the lanky, drawling man making a cruel smirk. "An' I'll bet you a new hat you buried both them boys, too."

"We did. What about Sam Logan?"

"Well, Deputy, I'm fixin' to tell you. Sam's a hired gun. He's been operatin' down south, sometimes in Arizona, sometimes over in New Mexico."

"Is he wanted?"

The cowboy's smirk faded and was replaced with a shadowy look of doubt. "I can't rightly say whether he is or not, Deputy. But he was. A few years back there was a thousand dollars on his hide."

"How did you and your pardner happen to recognize him yesterday?" Perc asked, watching the drawling range rider closely.

"Oh, we used to work the same range he did. That was a year or so back. We'd know him all right. Everybody down around Wolf Hole'd recognize Sam Logan."

Perc stiffened. Wolf Hole. That was where John Reed was from; he'd said so himself. It dawned very gradually on Perc that it was no coincidence—Logan riding in one week and John Reed arriving the next week. He lifted his left arm and pointed with it toward the onward jailhouse. "March, mister," he said.

The cowboy looked over his shoulder, saw the jailhouse door, and looked back again with a shake of his head. "Not me, Deputy," he drawled. "I got a phobia about bein' inside jailhouses."

"March anyway," stated Perc, his right fingers closing around the .45 on his hip. "Maybe this one'll cure your phobia."

The cowboy smiled very softly. "Tried to do you a good turn," he drawled, not budging an inch. "Sure an ungrateful little town you got here." The man thrust his jaw out. "Look behind you, Deputy."

Perc felt like swearing. He knew what was behind him in the dusty night before he even turned. There were two of them, Ev had told him that, so had Sam Logan. So, in fact, had the sneering man in front of him. He sighed and turned. The other one was standing blanketed in gloom in the recessed doorway of the saddle shop. He had a naked six-gun low in his right hand, pointing straight at Perc's back.

"No hard feelings, Deputy," the drawling man said as Perc faced forward again. "All we was tryin' to do was place you in a position to maybe pick up a little extra spendin' money for Sam Logan. Now don't go 'n' do nothin' foolish when I walk off, Deputy. We got nothin' ag'inst you at all. Just tried to do you a neighborly favor is all."

Perc did not do anything foolish. He didn't do anything at all except turn and take a long look at the other one standing back there out of sight of the roadway covering Perc while his friend strolled off. Neither of them had sore right arms. The one he'd faced had been wearing only an old, faded blue butternut shirt; there had been no bandage under it. The one in the doorway was holding his .45 in his right hand. There was nothing wrong with that one, either.

Those two, then, were obviously not Doc Farraday's callers of the evening before. He thought of something else, too, as the second one stepped forth from his recessed doorway and started tiptoeing backward into the darker night. Ev had said they were floaters, drifters passing through on their way north. Well, obviously they hadn't floated or drifted. Obviously they were hanging around the Ballester country.

He turned and went on down to the jailhouse, entered, and looked over where Doc Farraday was standing by the stove, lighting a stogie. Farraday waved his hand over toward the desk.

"There's the one I worked on," he said, puffing. "The other one's probably also in that stack, but as I told you, he was out by my tie rack and it was too dark for me to get a look at him."

Perc stepped over, picked up the poster, and considered the tough, iron-eyed man staring back at him from the flyer. "Charley Ringo," he read aloud. "Wanted in Arizona ... five hundred reward. Wanted in Texas ... five hundred dollars. Wanted in Kansas ... five hundred dollars."

"He's valuable," murmured Farraday, strolling over to peer across Perc's shoulder at the black-eyed, swarthy, thin face looking back at them. "Murder, mail robbery, jail break. Nice fellow."

Perc put the poster aside, sat down at his desk, and began going through the posters. Farraday watched a moment, then said: "What're you doing? I told you, the other one …"

"There is someone else I'm looking for," said Perc, flicking the posters over as he glanced at them. "I just met this one outside the jailhouse a few minutes ago. He had a pardner with him, too. Seems nowadays they just don't travel alone any more."

Farraday watched a moment, then headed for the door. "If you don't need me any further, I'll be getting along."

"I'm obliged," muttered Perc, turning the posters over one at a time. "Thanks ever so much, Doc."

Farraday departed.

Perc went completely through the stack without finding the cowboy he'd met a few moments earlier outside on the dark plank walk. He leaned back, felt around for his tobacco sack, and bent his head as he scowlingly worked up a smoke. It didn't make a whole lot of sense, whatever was happening in Ballester. There had to be some connecting link, had to be some reason or explanation, but it quite eluded him.

The disappearance of Sam Logan worried him the most. Patently those two informers, whoever they were and whatever their purpose was in hanging around town after indicating they were just passing through, hadn't known Sam had left town when they'd stopped Perc outside. And yet Perc was sure that Logan had pulled out long before, probably about the same time Perc had also left town early in the morning.

But why? Of course Sam had said he was going to leave, but he'd indicated he wasn't going to do it for several days yet. And the wounded man? He also had to be somewhere around, according to Doc Farraday who was an undeniable authority on gunshot wounds, but where?

The door opened and Everett Champion walked in, his expression troubled. "I've been looking around for you all day," he grumbled, closing the door and stepping away from it. "You remember those two drifters who came in and told me about Logan?"

"Yeah, I remember," said Perc, taking a big drag off his cigarette. "Only they weren't drifters. They're still around town somewhere."

Champion's face smoothed out. "Oh, you talked to 'em."

"Well, sort of, Ev. A kind of one-sided conversation. What about them?"

"They came into my place this afternoon and hung around until about an hour ago."

"Until they saw me ride back into town," mused Perc. "What'd they have to say this time?"

"Nothing. They just drank and loafed and wandered around the place. I kept clear of them. And there's something else. Whatever you said to Logan last night must've worked like a dose of salts. He moved out this morning and hasn't even shown up over at Ab's place."

"That's what you fellows wanted, isn't it?"

"Yes," assented the sly-eyed older man. "I'm not complaining, Perc. I just thought I'd tell you about those first two … and let you know whatever you told Logan worked."

"Thanks," Perc dryly said, got up, and went over to the door. As he opened it, he said: "Anything else?"

Champion looked a little bewildered as he shook his head and walked out of the office.

Perc stepped back to his desk, picked up that second poster, pocketed it, blew out his desk lamp, and walked out, turned to padlock his jailhouse door, and turned right as he strode away.

He had one more thing still on his mind in the realm of unfinished business. John Reed. Reed had made him wonder a little the evening before. Several things that had crystallized since that time had firmed up into a hard suspicion of Reed, and now Perc had in mind putting aside his soft gloves with Reed.

Reed and Sam Logan knew each other. He'd bet a year's wages on that. He'd been to Wolf Hole, Arizona. It was a well and a peach tree at the side of the road. No two men such as Logan and Reed, in a place no larger than Wolf Hole, had escaped seeing each other. Yet, here in Ballester, they acted as though neither had ever before set eyes upon the other.

And another thing, if these other strangers who were also drifting mysteriously into Ballester knew Sam Logan, then they also knew John Reed. The whole thing had a bad smell to it. When this many gunmen and outlaws drifted into a cow town, there had to be a very good reason for it, and that was precisely what he meant to sweat out of John Reed right now—this very night.

He cut through Ab's barn and turned northward up the yonder alleyway. It was only slightly less dark than it had been the evening before, but the alley was just as deserted as it had been then. That same orange glow came from the Reed wagon. He walked straight toward it.

CHAPTER NINE

Abigail came to the door when Perc knocked. She had her hair down and a light shawl around her shoulders. She recognized him at once and neither smiled nor spoke as she waited.

"I'd like to see your paw, if I can," he said, not at all impervious to the affect of her wealth of wavy brown hair and the way it framed her face.

"He's not here, Mister Whittaker. He was gone when I came back from the general store. I haven't the least notion when he'll be back." She paused, watched the way he accepted this information, then said: "Is there anything I can help you with?"

He slowly shook his head. What he was thinking was elemental. Reed hadn't left Ballester since his arrival in town more than a week earlier. Now he just happened to pick the same day to ride out that Sam Logan had also picked.

"Mister Whittaker ... what is it?"

He looked up again. She had read his puzzlement and his doubts even in that poor light. Before he could reply, she stepped through the door and came down the little stand of rough steps to the ground in front of him. It was a very warm night but in spite of that she drew the shawl closer about her shoulders. When she tipped back her head all that thick, heavy hair cascaded around her full shoulders.

"It's about my father, isn't it?" she persisted, holding the shawl close and staring up at him. "Isn't it, Mister Whittaker?"

"No," he finally said. "It's nothing to get upset about, Miss Abigail. I just wanted to talk to him is all. I didn't know he wasn't around. Where do you reckon he might be?"

She didn't answer that but instead stepped closer to search his face, to make certain he wasn't just trying to shield her from something. Evidently what she saw reassured her for she loosened her hold on the shawl and settled slightly, letting the stiffness depart.

"I have no idea where he went. I don't even know why."

Over beyond them at the public corral two horses squealed and lunged at one another. Beyond the corral, farther off but distinctly visible, light from the Golden Slipper lay in warm square patterns out in the roadway. He took her elbow and strolled over to lean upon the cribbed old corral poles with her. Out there, away from the wagon's shadow, moonlight touched her. He felt in a pocket, drew forth a folder, carefully smoothed it out, and draped it across a peeled-pole stringer. "Know him?" he asked, and closely watched her reaction as she leaned a little to study the vicious, swarthy face on that Wanted poster.

She straightened up and shook her head. "No. I'm sorry but he's not at all familiar."

Perc was disappointed. He'd felt confident her father would have recognized that outlaw, and after discovering Reed wasn't around, he'd thought she might know that man, too. He slowly re-folded the paper and tucked it away. She kept watching him all through this.

Finally she said: "What is it, Mister Whittaker, what's bothering you so much?"

"Logan left town today," he answered. "Now I want you to tell me something."

"If I can."

"Tell me John Reed didn't know Sam Logan."

She hung fire a moment over her reply, then she said: "Mister Whittaker, you're cynical. I've never seen that in you before. It surprises me. No, I can't say my father didn't know Sam Logan because he did. They knew each other very well."

He stared at her. She gave him look for look, never flinching or wavering. When he loosened and reached out to lay an arm upon a corral stringer, she moved to place her shoulders against the same stringer, facing away from the yonder roadway and instead toward the western run of land.

"Sam Logan was the lawman who sent my father to prison, Mister Whittaker. That was a long time ago. I was just a girl when it happened."

He blinked and looked down at her again. "Logan … a lawman?"

"Yes. What did you think … a gunfighter? Well, in a way he was, but not in the way you've thought of him."

"I'll be … Ma'am, that fellow I showed you the picture of … are you absolutely certain you've never seen him before?"

"I'm sure, Mister Whittaker. If I had, I'd have told you."

"He came into town last night with a bullet in him. Doc Farraday said he couldn't have gone far after he patched him up. Do you suppose Logan could've seen that man … could want him for something or other?"

She made a little shrug. "Sheriff Logan's been retired several years, Mister Whittaker. He only came out of retirement because my father sent for him down at Wolf Hole in Arizona."

"I see. What's your father up to?"

"I'm sorry, Mister Whittaker. You'll have to talk to him about that."

"But you know?"

"Yes, I know."

"And you knew Sam Logan, too?"

She nodded. "He was sitting on a bench in front of the livery barn when we drove into town. He told us last night he'd been sitting on that bench long enough to hatch a setting of eggs."

"Whoa," murmured Perc. "Last night. Do you mean just before I came along to talk to your pappy, he was at the wagon?"

"Yes. In fact, he left just a few moments before you came up."

So that's who that blurry shadow had been. Perc felt like kicking himself. He'd thought at first, from the size, it was Abigail. Logan was taller than Abigail, but walking stealthily and stooped, he wouldn't have appeared any taller in the darkness.

"Sam hasn't wanted to risk coming to see my father before. He said, after those two cowboys forced him into gunfights, he was no longer the nondescript drifter he'd hoped the people around Ballester would think, he said they'd be watching him."

Perc hooked both arms over the corral and leaned there, gazing over across the roadway toward Ev Champion's saloon. A lot of things were falling very neatly into place.

Abigail half turned and gazed at his bronzed profile. "Let them work it out, Mister Whittaker. It's something my father feels that he must do, and it is also something Sam Logan has to do."

"Kill each other," said Perc, turning to face her. "Two old men with a big, out-dated grudge coming this far to square an old-time …?"

She laughed. First she looked startled, then she laughed. It was a soft, rich laughter, lifting into the warm night and sounding full of relief. He stopped speaking.

"No, Mister Whittaker, it's nothing like that at all. They're *friends*, not enemies. My father told you … I've also told you … he's a changed man. He's neither an outlaw any longer nor a vengeful man. They are in this together but as friends. Please believe me."

He continued to watch her for a moment. The relief and the amusement stripped her of ten years. Or maybe it was just the silvery star shine that did that, but for the first time since he'd known her, Abigail Reed was a girl again. He dropped both arms and turned, leaned upon the corral, and said: "Just for a minute there I almost forgot those two, Abigail."

She became instantly cautious and wary, her soft, liquid glance both distant and at the same time warm toward him.

"If you'd tell me what it's all about, maybe I could keep someone from getting hurt, ma'am."

"No. As I've already said, Mister Whittaker, let them do it their way."

"It's got something to do with these strangers showing up in town, hasn't it?"

She looked straight at him and did not answer. She brushed away a heavy wave of hair and looked over toward the wagon where a lantern glowed. She was not going to say any more on this subject. Moonlight touched down into the V of the throat, showing an erratic pulse.

He put out a hand to her. She neither moved clear nor resisted his touch. The night before when he'd made this a personal matter between them, she'd told him good night and had walked away. Now, she stood like stone, not even looking at him, her eyes fixed dead ahead, her face entirely unreadable.

He stepped away from the corral, lay both hands upon her waist, half swung her toward him, and drew her inward.

She came forward and stood on tiptoes as his head dropped, cutting out the sickle moon overhead and the rash of stars. He found her lips and suddenly she was against him, meeting his hunger with a strong, quick fire of her own, and whatever had been between them before was gone in that instant. In its place was something altogether new, something a little frightening, a lot confusing, and quietly solemn.

She braced with both palms against his chest, exerting slight pressure. He eased back and raised his head. As before, she met his glance head-on in her characteristically frank and candid manner.

"It was too easy, wasn't it?" she whispered to him.

"It was hard," he replied, "very hard … not to."

She dropped back down, turned, and put both arms around an old corral post, stood a while considering the restless horses inside the public corral, then said: "Now things are different between us. Percy, I think we'll be sorry about that."

He put up a hand to touch her hair, let the hand lie lightly upon her shoulder. "Different all right, Abbie, but it'll take a heap of convincing to make me sorry."

"You don't know."

"And," he murmured, leaning beside her, also gazing in at the horses, "I don't care."

"Even if I won't help you against my father and Sheriff Logan?"

"Abbie, that belongs to another world. Another part of my life. This … what happened here just now … this belongs to a part of me that's got nothing to do with badges and guns, and trouble."

She turned to gaze at him. "My father said you were different. Sam Logan also said that. They like you, Percy. Neither of them is an easy man for other men to fool."

He looked down and met her upturned face. "All the same I wish … in one way … they'd taken their feud, or whatever it is, to some other town."

"They couldn't. They didn't have anything to do with making the arrangements. Other men did that. They only trailed along."

He smiled down at her. "Sometimes you make more sense than any woman … or man … I've ever known. Other times, like now, you talk in plain riddles."

She returned his smile. "I don't think tonight it's important, is it?"

He chuckled and wagged his head, stepped back, and felt for her hand. "Tonight nothing's important to me … but you." He started back over toward the wagon with her, pacing slowly and feeling the solid rhythm of her cadenced walk beside him, saw how the heavy cascading waves of her hair caught and entrapped vagrant moonbeams. "Last night I guess I sort of took you by surprise, saying those things to you."

She gave him an impish little smile. "Not exactly. I just had other thoughts last night. But I knew before that, Percy. I knew that day you helped me fill the water barrel. A woman feels things like that. She doesn't have to be told."

They halted near the wagon. Over across the vacant lot and beyond the community corral a cowboy hooted, long and loud, at another range rider and got back a simulated coyote wail that sent both those unseen men into peals of good-natured laughter. She heard and looked over that way and said: "It's a good town. We both like it."

Perc nodded but said nothing because he'd recognized the voice making that coyote wail. Boots, the *cocinero* for Snowshoe. If Boots was in town, then so also were the other Snowshoe men, including Johnny West, and that also meant something else—John Reed's identity was in a fair way to becoming public property. He sighed a little and said: "Abbie, by morning folks are going to know your paw's not someone named Jonah Reeves."

"It had to happen, didn't it, Percy?"

He nodded. Yes, it had to happen, but it didn't have to happen tonight because it depressed him, and this was the one night of all nights he didn't want to be reminded of all the intricacies of life. Just for a little while he wanted to go back to a time when the stars were closer, the moon brighter, the fragrance stronger, the way they had all seemed to him as a small boy.

"I reckon I'd better go now, Abbie."

"I suppose you must."

He reached for her. She came swiftly and hungrily. She found his mouth and burned him with her passion, threw him a little off balance with her unleashed fire, then dropped down and stood, pale and dark-eyed, before him.

"It was the same with me, Percy, that day down beside the creek. I wanted you to know. Good night."

She moved past, went up into the wagon, and eased the door closed after she entered. He could still smell the fragrance of her hair and feel the ripeness of her mouth and was therefore unwilling to move away for a while. Eventually, though, he turned and walked down toward the rear entrance to Ab Fuller's livery barn. Up near the roadway entrance, Ab's recognizable silhouette was engaged in conversation with another man, a second shadow that was thoughtfully puffing on a long cheroot.

Perc didn't feel much like being engaged in talk by those two, so he turned and strolled on down toward the jailhouse. The alley was empty and quiet.

He came out upon the yonder roadway near the saddle and harness shop where he'd earlier walked into the harmless little ambush with those two strangers, and this location brought his thoughts back to other things.

He knew more than he'd known before he'd gone to the Reed wagon, but he didn't know enough. Still, he'd made a good start. Come morning, he'd nail John Reed and get the rest of it—one way or another.

CHAPTER TEN

A man's best plans are never entirely dependent upon the planner. Reed did not return to town in the night. Abbie told Perc that after he'd around the town, looking for Reed and Logan. She was worried, she said calmly, but not too worried. She smiled into his eyes and said if ever two men were capable of looking out for themselves it was her father and Sam Logan.

Perc went around to Ab's barn and asked if the parson had rented a horse. Ab's reply indicated that exactly what Perc had prognosticated the night before had come to pass. With a narrowed look Fuller said: "Parson, hell. You mean John Reed, the outlaw. That's who that fuzzy-faced old coot is … in case you hadn't heard, Perc."

"I'd heard, Ab. What I want to know is did he rent a horse from you yesterday?"

"Yes he did. A good gray gelding. It'd take a good horse to pack him around." Ab paused and squinted closely at Perc. "You knew? You mean you knew all the time he wasn't no parson? Them Snowshoe fellers over at the saloon last night said you didn't know nothing."

"Nice to have friends like that," murmured Perc, looking across at the Golden Slipper's empty tie rack and closed front doors. "Sure I knew. Something else I know you might like to spread around town, Ab. Sam Logan's not a professional gunfighter like rumor has it. He's a lawman. At least he's a retired lawman."

"Ahhh," croaked Fuller, popping his eyes wide open. "A lawman? Are you dead certain, Percy?"

"Yeah. Now about this gray horse. What time did the parson ride out on him?"

"Two o'clock in the afternoon."

"Say where he was going?"

"No."

"Which way did he ride?"

"Northward, up the back alley, then he cut off westerly like he was heading for Snowshoe, or at least like he was bound for Snowshoe range."

Perc thought a moment, then said: "Rig out my horse. I'll be back for him in a minute." As he strode southward toward the jailhouse, he knew Ab was standing back there, scratching his head and peering after him. Ab scratched his head whenever he was perplexed.

Perc got a Winchester carbine from his office wall rack and returned to the barn with it. Ab had his horse saddled and bridled. He stood aside, watching Perc buckle the carbine boot into place and he sucked his teeth until Perc turned the horse, mounted, and evened up his reins. Then Ab said: "Deputy, what you up to?"

Perc smiled enigmatically and told the simple truth. "I don't know, Ab. See you later."

He rode out of town with a brassy orange disc climbing steadily upward from off in the diamond-clear east. Where the stage road made a little dog-leg jag, he left it, heading west. He rode back and forth, seeking a particular set of tracks, but because many horsemen had come and gone in this area there was nothing to set a course by. He therefore set his course straight for the Snowshoe headquarters ranch.

By the time he came within sight of those distant buildings, the sun was high and hot, the land lay cowed, and the few little straggles of cattle he passed were bunched up under whatever shade they could find.

As he passed down into the Snowshoe yard, someone bawled out a blistering string of profanity over behind the barn and dust spurted around there. He angled his mount over for a look. Three men were branding calves in a big circular corral, one at a fire over near the big gate, and the others on horseback with their ropes down and ready. The man at the fire had just inadvertently grabbed up a hot iron without his gloves and had been burned. He was no longer cursing when Perc came around the barn, but he had his injured hand plunged wrist deep into a nearby bucket of water.

There was a fourth man there, but he was on the outside of the corral, casually looking in. At the sound of an approaching rider he turned and looked. It was Snowshoe's range boss, Johnny West. The minute he recognized Perc he stepped back from the corral and waited.

Perc dismounted and strolled on over. One of the horsemen made a little backhand loop. Perc stopped to watch. The rope settled neatly around the head of a two-hundred-pound bull calf full of bawl and battle. The second the dallies were taken, the rope snapped taut, the calf exploded with an angry and terrified bellow. As his hind legs left the ground, a second rope snaked out and under, caught both legs, and sang taut. The calf fought on even after he was upended and being dragged to the fire where the grimacing rider with the burned hand picked up a wicked-bladed knife and stepped forward.

"Good roping," Perc said casually to Johnny West. "Takes me back a few years."

West smiled in recollection. He and Perc had done the team roping in those days, and like all men who worked together long enough, they got so that each complemented the other. "Yeah. Sometimes I wish those years were back again, Perc. Being boss takes a lot of the fun out of it."

"I reckon so," murmured Perc, and turned. "Johnny, how many strangers have you seen on Snowshoe range lately?"

"Strangers? None, Perc. At least, if the boys have seen any, they haven't said anything about it. Why, you got some kind of trouble?"

"Some kind, yeah, but I don't know exactly what kind, Johnny. There are four hardcases on the range somewhere. Six really, but I'm only interested in four of them."

West made a wry face, saying: "That doesn't make much sense, Perc. How about the other two?"

"John Reed and Sam Logan. I'm not too interested in them right now, except that I figure wherever the others are, Reed and Logan might also be."

West's expression hardened a little. "I don't know anything about the first four, Perc, but if I was you, I'd sure look out for those last two. Reed's a …"

"Johnny," broke in Perc in a dry tone, "Reed's served his time and been set free. Regardless of what old Boots thinks, that's the fact of the matter."

"Like I said, Perc, an old dog is still an old dog."

"I hope you're never put in a bad spot," retorted Perc, annoyed a little. "It's pleasanter to be a judge than to be the judged. As for Sam Logan … I thought I'd ride out and tell you another fact, Johnny, just in case you or Boots or any of your men get mean ideas. Logan's a retired sheriff from down in Arizona."

West got the same look of astonishment on his face Ab Fuller had also gotten. "A lawman? You mean that tough little cuss with his pearl-handled .45 isn't a gunfighter?"

"That's what I mean, Johnny. Pass the word around. Not that I figure any of your buckaroos are foolish enough to want to get planted like Banning and Johnson, but just so's, if they see either Reed or Logan on the range, they'll let you know right away. And you let me know."

West looked back over where the two ropers were laughing

because that hefty bull calf—no longer a bull but still full of fight—had just upset the man working the marking fire, and the upset man was turning the air blue with his anger and profanity.

When West looked back, he said: "You plumb sure you're right about all this, Perc?"

"Plumb sure, Johnny."

"All right. I'll pass the word, and if anything comes of it, I'll either ride into town and let you know, or send someone in. Anything else?"

"No," replied Perc as he mounted his horse, turned, and rode northward out of the Snowshoe yard. He turned once, a hundred yards out, and gazed back. Johnny was still standing where Perc had left him, gazing northward.

The heat got fierce after high noon. June, July, and August were hot months. It usually didn't begin to cool off in uplands Utah until about the middle of September. The heat lay in gelatin-like waves that eddied and broke as a man passed through them. Even the shade was rarely pleasant and the water holes were tepid and rimmed around by a green scum. The water wouldn't kill a man, but it sure didn't improve him any. Perc got thirsty long before he got across the Snowshoe range up toward the more broken, jagged northward country where the big Rainbow outfit grazed. He knew the country well and headed straight for a spring near a clump of rough-barked, old, shaggy junipers. When he finally got there, though, he held his horse back from the water and sat perfectly still atop his horse.

A dead man lay half in, half out, of the water hole. Except for the nearby junipers, the land was more or less open in all directions. He looked for a long time, making a careful study of every rock and tree and broken stretch of land. Nothing moved. There was no loose horse standing around and in the overhead brassy sky no buzzards circled.

He finally dismounted, walked in a little closer, and kneeled, holding his impatient horse back from the water while he studied the ground.

Two horsemen had ridden to this spot. They had dismounted, gone ahead to drink, and while one stood back, evidently holding their animals, one had flopped belly down to drink. Perc shook his head; every now and then an outlaw got careless like that. Every once in a while someone misplaced his trust. There was nothing to tell him what had happened next, but there didn't have to be. That dead man with his face in the water had a little scorched hole through his shirt right between his shoulder blades, plumb center. The other one, the man holding the horses, had simply drawn his .45, aimed, and fired. As simple as that. He had then mounted up and ridden off, leading the dead man's animal.

Perc stood up, went ahead and dragged the body clear, let his horse move around and drop its head to gulp water, while he rolled the corpse over. It was the same man who'd laughed in his face when he'd ordered him to march into the jailhouse. The same cowboy whose likeness he had gone through his pile of Wanted posters last night, looking for, and whose likeness he'd never found.

He rummaged the man's pocket but someone had beaten him to everything except some small change and an old knife with a badly nicked blade. There was no wallet, no letters, nothing at all to identify the dead man. He stood up. He'd been thirsty until now. He turned slowly to study the position of the sun, the flowing land, those tracks heading off southeasterly, and decided it would be useless to try and trail the other one so late in the day.

He got the corpse across his saddle, lashed it down, mounted behind the cantle, and turned back for town. The horse plodded and the sun beat down mercilessly. He tried to make sense out of the murder and could only come up with one plausible explanation. The killer, knowing Perc had seen his dead partner and would probably remember him, had perhaps decided that the best way to resolve any trouble that might accrue from their meeting was to kill his partner.

It was pretty weak, he told himself, on the ride back toward Ballester, but he had nothing else to go on—yet. He also thought

Logan and Reed might know this man. Even if they didn't, he was grimly certain they would know something, why this man and his friend were in the country, who those other two were—the wounded one and his companion. Surely something.

He didn't come into sight of town until after sunset. On a horse carrying double under sizzling July heat no sensible man ever tried to set any speed records. It was just as well, he thought, riding into Ballester with a corpse was certain to stand the town on its ear.

He didn't go down the main road but came into the rear alleyway from the west, by-passed Ab's barn, and got all the way to his jailhouse without encountering anyone. It was suppertime. Ballester was quiet and serene. He unloaded his grisly burden and locked it inside a little shed out back, led his horse up to the livery barn, and was relieved when the hostler who came out to get his animal informed him Ab had gone over to the café for supper.

He next went to Doc Farraday's place, got the medical man to accompany him back to the shed out back, brought a lantern from the jailhouse, and showed Farraday the dead man. The doctor kneeled and made a cursory examination, stood up and said: "Right through the heart from the back, Deputy. Is that what you wanted to know?"

Perc looked wry. "I'm not blind, Doc. I saw where the slug hit him. What I want to know is why … and you can't answer that. Otherwise, I want to make you a present of him."

Farraday looked down and said: "I'm sure of one thing. He's not either of the men who came to my place last night, Perc."

"How can you be sure he's not the one who was on the horse?"

"Easy. He's not as tall as that one was."

They went back out into the warm night. Perc re-locked the shed and straightened up to glance along the alleyway up where orange lamplight shone through the upper square of glass in John Reed's wagon's rear door.

Farraday said: "Have you any idea who did it, Perc?"

"I think so, Doc. There were two of them. I met them last night.

I don't know who they were and I didn't get a good look at the other one." Perc turned, blew out his lantern, and said: "How about the feller who was hurt, will he come back to have his bandage changed?"

Farraday considered this a moment, then shook his head. "No. He might need more care but he won't be back. Anyone who'd ride as far as he'd ridden before seeing a doctor wouldn't be likely to return for more care when his wound was beginning to heal. I'll tell you, Perc, you've got a big problem. There's something going on around here. I can't even guess what it might be, but I can tell you this much, that man in there was cut from the same bolt of dirty cloth as the man was with the bullet hole in his arm. Outlaws, pure and simple. Well, I've got to go finish supper. I'll send someone around for this one in the morning. Good night."

"Good night, Doc, and thanks."

Farraday's stooped figure shuffled away up the alley. Perc stood, holding his unlit lantern gazing straight up where John Reed's wagon stood. He turned finally, put aside the lantern, and struck out straight up through the gloom for the wagon.

CHAPTER ELEVEN

It was his third visit to the wagon but persistence paid off. When he knocked, John Reed opened the door and looked down at him. Reed's face was sunburned and freshly scrubbed, but the eyes were tired and a lot of their piercing quality was lacking as he gravely considered Perc Whittaker.

"You're a hard man to keep track of," said Perc. "Step down here, Mister Reed, I want to show you something."

Reed came out, closed the door, and didn't open his mouth as Perc turned and started walking down the dark alleyway. There was no spring in his step, though, and his thickly powerful shoulders sagged. Obviously John Reed was bone-weary. When Perc passed the spot where they'd previously stopped to talk, the bearded older man shot him an inquisitive look, but he still said nothing.

Perc picked up his lantern, re-lit it, unlocked the shed door, and motioned for Reed to enter first, which the older man did, but it was a tight fit—whoever had built that shack hadn't figured on a man of Reed's dimensions ever entering through that doorway.

Perc held the lantern high, closed the door, and put his back to it. Reed saw the dead man at once. He stood like stone, gazing into the sightless eyes before he finally made himself go forward, drop to one knee, and look closer. When he saw the exit hole of that deadly bullet, he drew back a sharp breath. To any experienced man a bullet hole was always larger and more ragged where it exited than where it entered. He turned his head very slowly and looked straight at Perc.

"From behind," he whispered. "Why, Deputy, why didn't you give him a chance?"

Perc blinked. "I didn't shoot him. I found him already dead. But you're right about that shot … it came from behind. Who was he, Reed?"

"Frank Rawlings," rumbled Reed, turning and dropping his head again.

"What was he?" Perc asked.

But Reed didn't answer. He kneeled there, hunched forward, looking more than ever like some old-time prophet with weak lamplight falling over his grizzled head and full, awry beard. "I asked *what* he was, Reed."

Old John stirred, heaved back, and got upright. He bent, still without speaking, and beat dust off his knee. As he afterward straightened around slowly, he said: "A cowboy. Not a very good one, but a range rider."

"Is that all he was?"

"No," muttered the older man, gazing straight down. "He was also an outlaw, Deputy. Never very good at that, either. He was working up to it, but he wouldn't ever have been in the class of the men who get their pictures printed on posters. Who killed him?"

Perc lowered the lamp. "There were two of them. Last night out front they tried to sic me on Sam Logan, hinted he was wanted by the law. I think they were trying to get me to lock Sam up on suspicion. Why, I'm not sure, but I think that's what they had in mind."

"Do you know where the other one is, Deputy?"

Perc shook his head. "I don't know who he is. That's why I brought you down here tonight, so you can tell me. There are a lot

of questions I want answers to, Reed. Maybe Abigail told you …
I've been looking for you and your friend, Logan."

"I can't tell you anything," rumbled the older man, shuffling
over closer to the door.

"You're going to have to," asserted Perc, planting his legs wide
and settling flat against the door. "There is another pair of these
men loose around Ballester."

Reed looked straight at Perc. "Describe them," he said, his deep
voice making a low growl.

"One of them has a bullet hole in his right arm," said Perc,
and fished for that Wanted poster. "This is who he is." He handed
the poster to Reed. "The other one wasn't recognizable in the dark
last night, but since I've never yet known an outlaw to be traveling
with anyone besides another outlaw, I think he'll have a price on his
topknot, too."

Reed bent and held the poster under Perc's lantern for a long, grim
moment while he studied the picture on it. As he slowly straightened
up and folded the flyer, he shook his head back and forth.

"As you know," he muttered, "this one is Charley Ringo. The
man with him in all probability will be Jim Howard."

Perc checked himself in mid-speech. Ringo and Howard! He'd
been surprised to learn from Farraday that the one with the wound
was Charley Ringo, but Jim Howard was one of the most wanted
desperadoes in the West. There was a $2,000 bounty on Howard
from Arizona alone. He'd been murdering and plundering his way
through life for seven years. There were other rewards, too, but
Arizona had the biggest one because it was down there that Howard
had committed most of his robberies and killings.

"What are these men doing in Ballester?" Perc finally asked, but
John Reed only looked down and shook his head. Perc waited, then
said: "Mister Reed, I'm giving you a choice. Either tell me what
this is all about, or get locked up." Reed raised his head. Outside
someone rapped softly, almost furtively, on the door. Perc shifted the

lantern to his left hand, drew his .45 with his right, and motioned for Reed to back away. Reed obeyed. Perc turned and said: "Who is it … what do you want?"

The answer came back, soft and difficult to make out through the door. "It's Doc Farraday again. I've got something to tell you."

Perc looked over where John Reed was stolidly standing, put up his gun, and reached for the latch. As he swung the door inward, Doc Farraday didn't enter. Sam Logan did, and Sam had a cocked .45 in his fist. Perc stood stockstill, letting his breath slowly run out. Logan gestured with his gun.

"Get away from the door, Deputy."

Perc stepped clear grimly and reluctantly. Logan's hat brim was tugged low, making a dark shadow over his upper face. Only the wet shininess of his rock-hard eyes showed clearly. "Been wondering who'd come out of here first," he said, speaking half to Perc, half to John Reed. "Got tired of the suspense. Take his gun, John." As Reed rolled forward, Logan shook his head slightly at Perc. "Don't be a fool, Deputy."

Perc had no intention of being a fool—or a dead hero, either, for that matter. He said: "How did you know Farraday had been here, Logan?"

"Saw him come down here with you, Deputy. That was after I saw you ride into town with Rawlings across your saddle. You shoot him, Deputy?"

Reed answered that as he moved back with Perc's gun in his hand. "It wasn't Whittaker. Rawlings came here with a friend. It was the friend who killed him. Whittaker just came onto Rawlings after he'd been salivated, Sam."

Logan stepped over and craned for a look at the dead man. "Sure enough Frank," he said. "Well, it's no big loss. He always wanted to be someone … now he is. But he had to get killed to get there." Logan looked at Perc and settled flat down in his boots. "Why couldn't you have just gone on being a nice cow-town deputy, Whittaker?"

Perc heard the drag of disappointment in Logan's voice and gazed at the smaller man. "Probably for the same reason you couldn't stay retired, Sam. A man sees things he should do and he tries to do them."

Logan looked at Reed and gently inclined his head. Reed nodded as though whatever thought had passed between them hadn't reached him unexpected. He shuffled forward with Perc's gun in his massive fist. "Sorry, son," he rumbled. "We don't mean you any harm. Only like Sam said, if you'd just gone along minding your own affairs, things would've worked out a lot better all around."

Logan said, speaking sharply: "Whittaker …!"

Perc turned. That was when Reed swung the gun barrel. Just for a thousandth part of a second Perc knew where he'd blundered, but before he could even gather himself to spring clear, the barrel crunched down across his head, blackness exploded from every direction, and he fell with a soft little rustling sound.

* * * * *

It was the cold that awakened him, the pre-dawn chill that seeped through the shed's warped and cracked old walls. He had a throbbing pulse of steady pain inside his head, but when he rose up and looked around, he saw the dead man lying there and remembered all that had happened, and the pain seemed to lessen slightly.

Still he was groggy for fifteen minutes after he got to his feet and sank down upon an old crate in the shed to wait for some of the dizziness to depart. His reflections were not very charitable. He'd pistol-whipped a few fractious souls in his time and resented the force of the blow that had struck him down. Even when he reasoned that a man as powerful as John Reed, when he lightly tapped someone over the head, was using as much force as a lesser man would possess when he swung with all his strength, didn't make him feel a whole lot better.

He finally felt well enough to stand up and was reaching for the door when it opened and Abigail appeared in the opening, looking white in the face and with her eyes as large as agates.

"My father left a note that you were in here … that I should come down and … What *happened* to you, Percy?"

He put out a hand to her. "Ask your father," he growled, and let her lead him out into the chilly new day gloom. "He hit me over the head, that's what happened to me."

She put a strong arm around his middle and guided him up the alley toward the Reed wagon. "You'll feel better in a little while. I'll make some fresh coffee and some …"

"What else did that note say?" he growled. "Where those two old catamounts have gone this time and what they're up to?"

All she said was: "Come along now and lean on me, if you want. You'll feel better after a while."

He did begin to feel better after he'd been moving. His headache faded a little, too, but he didn't tell her so. She helped him up into the wagon. It was spacious and well furnished. At the forward end a partitioning length of bright cloth hung down, but in the rear of the wagon there was a crackling little iron stove. He stood with his back to that blessed heat while gingerly exploring the top of his head. She watched him do this while ladling water from a cask into an old graniteware coffee pot, and said: "It's fortunate you have such thick hair, Percy."

"That danged old coot," he growled, feeling the lump. "He didn't have to hit *that* hard."

She was fully clothed but hadn't bunned her hair yet. As she moved, it swirled in beautiful waves around her shoulders. He stopped feeling the bump and sank down upon a small bench.

"Abbie, would you do something for me?" he asked.

She turned from the stove without smiling but with a softness to her glance that was both a smile and a promise. "Yes. What is it?"

"Don't put up your hair. Just let it lie like it is now."

She laughed. Her whole face brightened with a soft pinkness. "But I'm a woman, not a girl, Percy. Women put up their hair."

"Just be a girl, then," he said, smiling up at her. "It's beautiful just like it is."

She turned back to the stove. "If you wish it," she told him, then cast a sidelong glance over. "You aren't mad at me?"

"You? Why you?"

"Well, it was my father who hit you over the head, wasn't it?"

He stopped smiling. "Yes it was the consarned old bushy-faced coot. But *he* did it, you didn't." He reached for the cup she held out to him. The coffee was black and it was hot. It was also some kind of liquid magic for within minutes after downing it his headache diminished until it was scarcely noticeable.

"Where did they go?" he asked, and knew from the way she went on working at the stove as though she hadn't heard that she wasn't going to answer.

"All right. What's their tie-in with Ringo and Jim Howard?"

This time she answered. "It's not what you think, Percy. It really isn't. But, as I've said before, this is their affair. I can't interfere and you shouldn't interfere."

"Abbie, honey, there's a dead man in that shed down the alley. There's nothing very funny about a dead man. This thing's got to come out into the open before there are more dead men."

She paled, but all she said was: "Fetch the bench over closer. Breakfast is ready."

CHAPTER TWELVE

He had scarcely begun to eat when a little insistent rap came on the door of Abigail's wagon, and she went to see who it was. He recognized the voice instantly and gulped the last of his coffee, arose, and stepped over to look out. Perhaps under different circumstances Ab Fuller would have looked inquisitive or shocked or just plain interested in the spectacle of those two at the door of the Reed wagon, but now he wasn't. He was anxious-faced and disturbed.

"Come along," he said when Perc appeared. "I've got to talk to you."

Perc edged around Abigail, felt for her fingers, squeezed them, let go, and sprang down out of the wagon. Ab turned at once and paced down the alleyway toward his barn. He didn't say a word until they'd turned up into the runway, then he spun around and said: "Perc, two horses were stolen from me last night. Taken right out of the barn."

Perc was interested at once but he didn't understand how Ab's thoughts were running until the liveryman pointed across at the two empty stalls. Both stalls were near the rear of the barn, close to the alleyway exit, and side-by-side. It looked to Perc like the case of a pair of men entering together, taking the first two horses they found that were side-by-side, and riding out.

"I figure it was John Reed, Deputy," stated Fuller. "He'd have reason to take the horses, and besides that, this here alleyway exit is right handy to his wagon."

Perc turned and looked up and down the opposing rows of stalled animals. There was not a gray among them. "Ab," he said, "why would Reed take two horses, why would he steal horses at all? You rented him the gray and you'd have rented him another one or two if he'd wanted them."

Fuller didn't attempt to argue with the lawman's logic; he simply shifted his mental stance and said glibly: "All right, it wasn't Reed then. It was Sam Logan."

Perc stepped to a wooden saddle rack, straddled it, and looked skeptically at Fuller. "You're shooting at the moon," he grumbled. "You've got a phobia about Reed and Logan, so anything that happens you're going to blame on them."

Ab blinked and lowered his brows. "What's a phobia?" he demanded, not quite sure he wasn't being grossly insulted.

"Never mind," evaded Perc, looking over where those empty stalls were. "Where was your night hawk?"

"Asleep in the harness room."

"Just how good were those two pelters?"

"Plenty good, Percy. I keep my best animals back down here so folks coming to rent a mount see the worst ones first. One of those stolen horses was a fine chestnut. The other was a blazed-faced bay with four white stockings halfway up his pasterns, as neat and flashy as anything you ever saw. Good, sound, expensive horses, and, by God, I want 'em back in as good a shape as when they were stolen, too."

Perc stood up slowly, speculating on someone's need for two fresh mounts. It wasn't difficult to imagine who, besides Reed and Logan, would have use for such animals. "I'll look around," he told Ab. "You rig out my horse. I'll be back for him in a little while."

He walked outside and saw Everett Champion unlocking his saloon doors across the road and northward. He speculated on the possibility of Everett's knowing something but gave it up because, as popular as the Golden Slipper was, he thought it very unlikely any outlaws who considered it likely they might be under surveillance would go there.

He thought he knew who'd taken Ab's horses, but it disturbed him that Ringo and Jim Howard had had the guts to be in town last night. Possibly, while he'd been lying unconscious, they'd been within a few yards of him. One thing he was sure of. Reed and Logan hadn't taken those animals. He thought he'd better start looking now in earnest. First, he'd make a sashay around Snowshow range, then he'd head on up north again, as he'd done the day before, and scout up Rainbow's range. Somewhere out there, for some reason he could only speculate about, Reed and Sam Logan were perhaps doing the same scouting.

He turned to go back after his mount, but a pair of range men trotting in from the north, leading a pair of horses turned him quickly back around again. He didn't know the riders except by sight; they'd hired on last spring with Mexican Hat, which controlled the eastward range. He knew just that much about the riders and no more.

They saw him standing out front of the livery barn and angled over to draw up in front of Fuller's tie rack. One of them bent, whipped a lead rope's shank around the rack, and said: "Deputy, couple of tucked-up strays we found northeast of town on Hat range. They sure had the hell ridden out of 'em. Looked to us like they was abandoned maybe last night."

Perc went forward and walked silently around the pair of horses. They were, as the Mexican Hat rider had stated, tucked up in the gut and flank, had brush scratches on them, and showed all the signs of having been pushed to the limit of their endurance and strength. "Where exactly did you come onto them?" he asked the cowboys.

"Northeast of town, maybe a couple of miles, but we back-tracked 'em a lot closer to Ballester. We figured, whoever set 'em loose, probably did it right here … maybe from the edge of town. They both got Arizona brands."

Perc looked up. "How do you know they're Arizona marks?" he demanded.

The Mexican Hat rider pointed at the shoulder of the nearest stray. "That there's Cross-Quarter-Circle, Deputy. I've seen it often enough. I used to work just north of the line down near Saint George. That Cross-Quarter-Circle outfit runs cattle on both sides of the line, but have their headquarters a few miles east of Wolf Hole, which is …"

"In Arizona," stated Perc dryly. "I know. Thanks a lot for bringing them to town, fellows. Next time we meet, I'll stand the drinks at the Slipper."

Both cowboys broadly grinned, nodded, and spun their mounts. Perc stepped back and gazed at the Cross-Quarter-Circle horses. For perhaps the hundredth time since taking the assignment as deputy sheriff at Ballester he wished the town possessed a telegraph office.

"Hey! Whose half-dead beasts are those?" Ab Fuller croaked, stepping out through the front of his barn, leading Perc's saddled horse. "People who'd abuse horses like that ought to be shot."

"I think, Ab, that's why they abused 'em like that. So they wouldn't get shot."

"What'd you mean by that?"

"Outlaws, Ab. Outlaws rode those horses hard and fast to escape a posse."

Fuller relinquished the reins of the horse he was holding to Perc and swung his wide-open eyes from the tie racked horses to Perc as the lawman checked his *cincha*, turned his horse once, and stepped up over leather. "You mean … say, Perc, I lost two, and someone abandoned two …?"

"Yeah. I've been thinking the same thing. Makes sense, doesn't it?"

"You going hunting for them?"

"Had that in mind, Ab. Take those poor devils inside. Stall 'em, cuff 'em down, and give 'em a good feed. I'll stand the cost."

Fuller turned and walked up closer to the tied animal. He locked his hands behind his back and walked back and forth, making a horseman's experienced appraisal. "You know, Perc, these've been darned fine beasts, young and tolerably sound and … by golly, I think I'll slap a line on 'em just in case."

"You do that," the deputy said, reined out, and swung to his left. The roadway was empty. Those two Mexican Hat riders had long since loped back toward their own range. It was too early in the morning for traffic yet. Some of the stores hadn't even been opened for business.

He reached the end of town, lifted his horse over into a comfortable lope, and pushed steadily ahead for a mile before swinging off westward. The sun was up but its heat hadn't risen as yet. There was an azure tint to the spotless sky, a good freshness to the air, and he scarcely remembered being struck over the head by John Reed the night before, with his own pistol.

Two things inclined him to believe the sorrow Reed had expressed the previous night about doing that to him. One was that note he'd left for Abigail, instructing her to help Perc. The other was the fact that, after belting him, Reed had replaced Perc's .45 in his hip holster. Neither act had been the move of an angry or antagonistic man. Rather they had been the acts of a man haunted by remorse and regret.

As he rode, he pieced together what he'd thus far figured out. It still left a big blank space, however, and the most logical conclusion he could use to fill that blank space in with was a rather obvious and unpleasant conviction that the old outlaw and the ex-lawman were definitely mixed up with a band of notorious renegades.

That's why, just before leaving town, he'd wished again for access to a telegraph office. He'd have wired Wolf Hole or its nearest adjoining town, which was St George, over the line in Utah, and ascertained if any lawless act had been committed in that area, by whom it had been committed, and perhaps learned if Charley Ringo and Jim Howard were involved in it.

He thought he knew the answer even without sending such a telegram. There *had* been some lawless act committed down there, and not only were Ringo and Howard involved, but so also were dead Frank Rawlings and the unknown outlaw with whom Rawlings had come north, and who had killed Rawlings at that Rainbow water hole.

The only fact he had trouble accepting was the illegal association of Sam Logan with a band of notorious murderers and thieves. Where John Reed was concerned, all he could do was earnestly hope. He didn't do that for Reed's sake; he did it for Abigail's sake. But still, deep down, he was almost certain Reed had lied to him about reforming, had also lied to Abbie, but with greater success. She believed in her father, a very natural thing, a sad thing, Perc thought as he headed for the upcountry range above Snowshoe's headquarters ranch. She'd had all the disappointments and anguish she deserved for one lifetime. When he met up with John Reed again, he meant now to tell him all the things he'd thought before but had refrained from saying to him.

The land lay dazzlingly clear and golden as far as he could see in all directions. Northward from Snowshoe, where the range began to heave and break up somewhat, there were more trees and clumps of sage and chaparral than occurred southward. But everywhere he looked, there was just the endless hush and stillness. Twice he spotted bunches of cattle drowsing in the shade, and once he startled a small band of pronghorn antelope. The handsome little goat-like creatures raised their flags, bristled their white rump hair, which was their warning signal, and sped away. The fastest horse living couldn't have even kept them in sight once they were alarmed.

He watched the antelope run, scuffing up a thin little banner of dust, slowed his mount to a walk after a mile of loping, and looped the reins to create a smoke. Suddenly he sighted distant movement far to the north of the disappearing pronghorns and froze. It wasn't a mounted man and it wasn't a four-legged critter. It looked to be somewhere in between. There were a few bears in the country but never this far southward from the mountains this time of year. Bears couldn't stand the scorching heat of midsummer without plenty of shade and water, of which there was not enough of either on the plains.

He forgot about the smoke, picked up the reins, and angled off to intercept whatever it was out there moving slowly southward. It was a man on foot. He saw that at about the same time the man sighted Perc and faintly called out at the same time, waving with both arms. He pointed his animal dead ahead and finally recognized old Boots, the Snowshoe *cocinero* and wrangler. Even before he was close enough for them to speak he could hear old Boots's fierce profanity.

He halted, swung down, and walked the last hundred yards, leading his horse. Boots was stumping along on his spindly, saddle-warped legs mad as a hornet but seemingly otherwise unhurt.

Perc stopped and let the *cocinero* cover the last hundred feet. "What are you doing out here on foot?" he asked, and triggered another withering blast of wrathful cursing.

"Pickin' posies," snarled the red-faced and sweaty wrangler.

"You get bucked off, Boots?"

"Yes, I got bucked off, dad-rat it. But if I'd had half a chance, it never'd have happened. There was a couple of fellers in a draw. I never seen 'em until they jumped up out of the arroyo like they was popping out of the ground. The consarned colt I was straddling took one look, bogged his head, and took to me like a brother. I lost one bucket, then the danged other one. I tried to find the horn but it was 'way downhill and I never got it, so I sailed away like a confounded bird and them two strangers like to fell down laughing, dang their mangy hides."

Boots was about to say more but Perc cut him off hard. "Where is this arroyo and what were they doing out there?"

"How the hell do I know what they were doing out there? By the time I got the cobwebs cleared out of my skull, they were riding off."

"In what direction?"

"Northward."

"Did you go look down in the arroyo?"

"Yes. They'd cooked their morning chow down there."

Perc eyed the wrangler's twisted, wrathful countenance. "Did Johnny tell you boys yesterday to report any strangers you met on the range?" he asked.

Old Boots sharply nodded. "He did. And I just now reported 'em, too. Now take me up behind your saddle and let's get back to the ranch."

Perc gazed off across the golden distance northward. He had no intention of wasting several hours taking Boots back to Snowshoe. It was a long walk, perhaps not less than five miles, but Boots would make it all right. He'd turn the air blue every inch of the way, but he'd make it.

Perc turned, got astride, hooked his horse into a lope, and sped away. Behind him Boots howled like a wounded eagle and shook his fists.

CHAPTER THIRTEEN

It was comparatively easy to backtrack the Snowshoe *cocinero*. He had a crabbed, little, hitch-a-long walk nothing else that walked or crawled could have successfully emulated. But when Perc came to that arroyo where Boots had been bucked off those tracks ended. He found the exact spot where the men had stood upon the edge of the arroyo as well as the place where Boots's Snowshoe horse had bucked him off.

Down in the arroyo was more sign than Boots had mentioned. Two men had tied their horses down there in the grass, had rolled out their bedrolls, and slept there. Evidently the two were Ringo and Howard, and if this were so, then they were now riding Ab Fuller's blazed-faced bay and his chestnut.

He'd originally anticipated that those two might have come up this way after stealing the horses, but what puzzled him as he went back and got astride was where Sam Logan and John Reed were. There was one possibility. Ringo and Howard meant to meet Logan and Reed, but not until after they were better mounted than when they'd arrived in the territory.

That made sense, Perc thought, reining off northwestward toward the distant hills following freshly shod horse tracks, it made sense for the basic reason that the prime element of any law of self-preservation west of the Missouri River was—always keep a fast, fresh horse under you. Life insurance was a good horse. There was no other kind of life insurance.

He rode for a solid hour with the sun striking hard down across his side and back, got well up into Rainbow's range, and finally halted to blow his horse in the pungent shade of a juniper tree. He made a smoke and surveyed the onward country. Those tracks he'd been following never deviated, never slackened. It was as though Ringo and Howard knew exactly where they were going. He speculated that they probably did, just because a band of renegades did not normally operate in a specific district meant nothing. In fact, clever and experienced outlaws usually held their meetings in places where people neither expected to see them, nor recognized them when they *did* see them. But Perc couldn't recall ever hearing anyone comment even in the most casual way about strangers being in the foothills of Rainbow range.

He killed his smoke and pushed on, struck the first slight rises in the land, and lost the tracks where a little narrow clear-water creek ran at the base of a swale. He puzzled over this. Not so much because the horsemen had obviously taken to the creek to hide their tracks, but that they'd bother doing this at all because, with the long start they'd had on him, they wouldn't have seen him following— unless, of course, they'd sat somewhere for a while, watching.

That, he decided, was entirely possible. Men like Jim Howard and Charley Ringo stayed alive only because they could out-wolf a lobo and out-Indian a bronco buck. He turned, let his horse pace along the northward flow of the creek, and watched the round- about countryside because this was ideal ambush country.

They'd gone north, he was confident of that. They'd been holding steadily to a northward course ever since he'd picked up their trail at the arroyo. The sun got hotter, the land drier except along his little gravelly creek, and up ahead were the middle-distance higher thrusts of the Ballester Mountains that weren't actually mountains, just heavy hills, but with nothing higher to compare them with for a good many miles they were called mountains.

He spotted two cowboys loping easily along, heading south-eastward in the general direction of Rainbow's home place, but he sat still in the curve of a slope until they were past. He wouldn't have taken them along, and if he hadn't done that, and they'd gone home, the whole Rainbow outfit would have come boiling out to see just what a lawman evidently on the hot trail was doing on their foothill range.

Later, rounding a curving hillside where a number of trees grew spottily, shielding him with their dense shade, he saw something else. It was a loose horse wearing both a saddle and a hackamore. Boots's colt.

He halted, sat for a long time watching as the colt grazed along as unconcernedly as though being this far north for a Snowshoe animal was the most natural thing under the sun. It wasn't. Snowshoe animals, whether they were cattle *or* horses, were rarely allowed to trespass on Rainbow grass. This, of course, worked both ways, that was how neighboring cattlemen in open-range country maintained their friendships.

The colt had evidently been either led this far or driven up here, and since Perc had been following only two side-by-side sets of shod horse marks, the colt hadn't been led.

The reasoning behind bringing Boots's colt this far was elementary enough. If the colt didn't amble toward home where his rider could perhaps catch him, no one down at Snowshoe—or anywhere else for that matter—would know a thing about two strangers in the land until all possibility of running them down was long past.

Perc dismounted, stepped over beside a tree, and leaned there. His horse paid no attention at all to the distant colt but dropped its head and began to browse.

This foothill country had never been used for anything but spring and early summer grazing. The earth was very shallow, full of gravel, and it dried out quickly after the heat came because four inches down was a layer of solid hardpan dynamite couldn't crack. For this reason no one used the foothills after summer came. In fact, since cattle didn't come up this far after full summer arrived, neither did any Rainbow cowboys. It was an ideal place for outlaws to rendezvous and Perc was satisfied that a rendezvous was somewhere in progress around here, or, if not right then in progress, was surely supposed to commence as soon as all the converging outlaws got in here.

Another factor inclining him toward his present conviction was the fact that neither Reed nor Logan had been able to get back to town, for a full day after initially riding out. They had obviously been at least this far away, and conceivably even farther, because so far, as near as Perc could make out, there was nothing to indicate the outlaws were congregating close by.

He started to turn, to reach back for the dragging reins of his horse, when a slow, steady movement snagged his attention upcountry about a mile where heat waves danced and got smoky. He straightened up and waited, watching that distant spot.

It was a rider, a cowboy, coming down through the twisting bends of those upcountry swales and slopes. He was riding a raw-boned bay horse and neither man nor animal appeared the least concerned with arriving any particular place at any particular time. They shuffled along through the midday heat like both were mechanically obeying some strong instinct.

Perc stepped back deeper into the shade of several bunched-up black oaks and caught his horse, tugged the beast closer, and kept a hand lightly atop the animal's nostrils to prevent a sound from breaking the heavy, hot stillness.

When the oncoming rider spotted the Snowshoe colt out there grazing, he stopped very abruptly and sat for a long time like stone. Perc knew exactly what the man was doing. He hadn't expected to see that loose horse out there and was now making a very meticulous examination of the round-about land. Perc did not fear detection, he was too securely safe in his gloomy shade, but it struck him that this rider, whoever he was, did not act like a Rainbow man would have acted. He was acting too wary, too cautious, to be someone with a legitimate reason for being where he was.

It crossed Perc's mind that this might be one of the rendez-vousing outlaws. But if it was, the stranger obviously hadn't met those other two—the ones who had brought Boots's horse this far north—or else he'd have expected to see the colt.

Finally, evidently satisfied no one was around, the stranger eased out, heading closer to the Snowshoe colt. Not until he passed from the yonder swale out into the full bright sunlight did Perc notice that the shuffling-footed bay horse he was riding wasn't just poking along, he was ridden-down and tucked-up, and that, at least, explained most of the stranger's quick, hard interest in the Snowshoe colt. He needed a replacement for the beast he was riding.

Perc watched the cowboy take down his rope, shake out a good loop, and hook it casually over his right shoulder as his horse walked steadily down toward the colt.

For some time, although he couldn't have failed to be aware of the oncoming rider, the colt went on grazing. But when he thought the rider was close enough, he raised his head and stared, both little ears up, his tail arched for a quick whirl and a swift run. He made a common mistake; he waited too long and underestimated the ability of the man, as well as the sixty-foot length of the man's lariat.

When the colt set back to whirl, the man was ready, for this is exactly what he'd been intently watching for. The minute the colt snorted, the man hooked his big bay hard, lunged ahead, made two big rising whirls with his lariat, and released it. The colt was still reversing when that big loop came high overhead and dropped with perfect precision. The colt was caught.

He fought. He plunged and bowed his head. He bawled and struck and bucked, but the cowboy had already taken his overlapping dallies. It was a losing fight. The big bay threw his weight backward and low, keeping his nose straight down the singing rope. Nothing that colt could have done would have saved him; he was caught and eventually he decided since this was emphatically so, there was little point in continuing the battle. That was when the man laughed. Perc heard it and almost smiled for the man; it was always a pleasant triumph to make a good throw and a better catch.

The man piled off and started down the rope hand over hand, but it wasn't necessary to be so cautious. Boots's colt was green-broken but he was broken, knew men, knew when it was useless to fight, and stood there, blowing, rolling his eyes a little, and softly snorting, doing all the customary things of a green-broke three-year-old, but only doing them because they were expected of him; he no more feared that oncoming man than he feared the sun or the moon.

But the man was cautious. He didn't know the colt, had reason to be careful and wary since the colt was wearing a hackamore, symbol of a green horse, and took his time. He knew what he was doing, Perc could see that easily enough. He could also see something else. Once that cowboy got astraddle, that colt, if he decided to try and pitch, was going to have a hard time unloading the stranger.

But the man talked his way on up and loosened his loop, freed the colt, tested the cinch of Boots's saddle, checked the colt, and swung up with all the sure grace and confidence of an old rough-string rider. The colt knew instinctively, as most green colts do, that he'd met his master. He made no attempt to buck or even drop his head. The man reined him out right and left, figure-eighted him, and swung him over by the bay. There, he dismounted, removed Boots's rig, and re-saddled the colt with his own outfit. After setting his tucked-up bay loose and waving him off, the stranger got back astride the colt and turned back the way he'd come.

Perc's understanding stare hardened a little at that. Evidently the stranger had been coming downcountry for the express reason of locating a fresh horse. Now he had one, there would be no

point in continuing his search. As the stranger headed back into
the onward hills, Perc turned also to get astride. He had good,
fresh tracks to follow. He was confident they would lead him to
wherever that secret meeting was to be held. As he waited for
the stranger to get far enough ahead so that it might be safe for
Perc also to cross that stretch of open country, he reflected a little
grimly that now all the outlaws were freshly mounted.

He got astride and sat a while without moving, speculating
on the distant stranger and turning grimmer with each moment
that passed. Since that man hadn't been either Charley Ringo or
Jim Howard, and since just as obviously he hadn't been either Sam
Logan or John Reed, he was the surviving member of that other
pair—Frank Rawlings and the man who had killed Rawlings with
a bullet in the back!

He ultimately drifted on down out of the shadows, struck the
hotly lit open country, and walked his horse steadily out toward
where the tucked-up bay was grazing. The bay saw him and raised his
head, but he was neither a colt nor a frisky horse and stood watching
with his head only a foot off the ground. Perc did not ride close; he
wanted the bay to stand perfectly still until he was parallel with him,
which the older horse obligingly did. Perc saw what he was seeking—a
Cross-Quarter-Circle brand on the bay's left shoulder.

He passed on by and picked up the colt tracks. Whoever owned
that Cross-Quarter-Circle outfit must be mad enough by now to
chew cannon balls and spit bullets. All these converging Arizona
bad men had raided his remuda for their mounts.

The colt's tracks were easy to follow because they were so fresh
that dust was still settling around them. But otherwise it might
not have been so simple because the colt was unshod and this was
a country where all loose horses were unshod, with footprints that
looked identical.

He got across into the yonder swale where the other man had
disappeared, left his horse tied in some chaparral, climbed a low

hill, and looked around from the top out. The rider was a mile farther along, riding toward a big bosque of cottonwood trees where, evidently, there was a spring or a water hole. The colt was behaving perfectly. He returned to his horse, got astride, and pushed onward. It was a little beyond high noon now, the heat was nearing its zenith, gelatin layers of sun smash danced ahead, the sky was a very faded, brassy blue, and what little shade lay along his route was confined around the base of trees and brush clumps.

There was one consolation to enduring this fierce heat. No one else, he thought, would be voluntarily riding out in it, so at least until he got closer to that bosque of cottonwoods he had little to worry about.

He began to speculate that John Reed and Sam Logan did not actually know where this rendezvous site was, otherwise by now he'd have seen them or would have at least cut their tracks. That puzzled him because it didn't fit in with his earlier notion that they were hand-in-glove with the outlaws. It also gave him fresh reason to hope he'd been wrong about them. If they were part of this outlaw crew, they'd surely know where the meeting was to take place.

CHAPTER FOURTEEN

He was plodding through a bare stretch of walled-in, heat-ridden smokiness when the unmistakable *clop-clop-clop* of a shod horse sounded ahead and off to his right where a small intersecting arroyo debouched upon the higher ground where he was. Each time one of those shod hoofs struck stone, the ringing sound was unmistakable. He looked frantically for a hiding place. There was none. He was completely exposed. Not a bush or a tree grew anywhere around. He thought this might be the outlaw riding that Snowshoe colt coming back for some reason, whisked out his carbine, stepped down, swung his horse across his own body, and laid the Winchester across his saddle seat. Sweat ran into his eyes, making them sting. His horse raised its head in curiosity and gazed over to where that little arroyo ended. It was a long, tense wait, then a loose horse ambled out of the arroyo, saw Perc's horse, and stopped to stare.

There were old saddle marks on that beast, and although it now seemed to have a comfortable gait, there were all the signs of much earlier hard riding about it. It bore that identical Cross-Quarter-Circle brand on the left shoulder and at one time had been a powerful, durable animal. Now though, like the bay back there and also like the pair of run-out horses back at Ab's barn in town, it was making a slow and painful recovery from much hard use and abuse.

Perc straightened up, stared a moment, pushed his saddle gun back into its boot, and stepped up over his own animal. He thought he knew whose horse that had been—Frank Rawlings's. He eased out and rode on up closer, did not slow as he went past but studied the horse minutely so he'd be able to remember it, then lost it when his mount took him on around into the next bisecting break in the onward trail.

A little way farther along his horse pricked up its ears. Even Perc caught the faint lift of coolness in the otherwise hot and arid atmosphere. There was water up ahead. They were nearing the cottonwoods and the water hole that usually was close by where such thirsty old trees grew.

But he tied his horse and scouted the onward trees afoot. Rawlings's killer had been heading for them, too. No one was around up there when Perc got far enough ahead to see the trees. The spot was as deserted and serene as though no one had ever been there. He went back for his horse. Farther back, that Cross-Quarter-Circle animal came ambling along as though also thirsty and bound for the spring, or else curious about Perc and wishing to have company.

Perc did a shrewd thing. He got behind the loose horse and drove it on ahead, let it amble up to the spring first, and waited to see what might occur. Nothing happened. From the way the Arizona horse acted, he knew the spring was uninhabited. His own horse was beginning impatiently to saw on the bit by then, so Perc rode on up and dismounted where a perfectly circular and glass-like pool of spring water lay. There was a little space of close-cropped greenery where the spring's lower end overflow dispersed making the grass grow. After drinking, the Arizona horse shuffled over there and dropped its head to eat.

Perc left his own mount and paced around, reading sign. Not too long before, perhaps very early that morning, two men had camped here. This puzzled him because the two that had gotten Boots bucked off couldn't have reached this spot so early. Upon the opposite side of the pool he found where two men had sat and smoked and left their sitting-down imprints as well as their cigarette stubs. These were even fresher marks. These two, he reasoned, would be the pair he'd been seeking before encountering that last man. All the tracks, when they left this shady, cool place, headed northwest, a totally different direction from which they'd all been riding up to now.

Then he saw the bleached cow skull with the arrow daubed on it with dried, black mud. The arrow pointed in the same direction those men had all ridden, after resting at this cottonwood spring.

He squatted in soft shade, made a cigarette for his noonday meal, and began to understand what was happening. Evidently these men had all been converging, patently enough, but just as clearly they didn't all know this uplands country and were following signs left behind by the first pair.

Two men had spent the night here. Two more had arrived this morning and had gone on. Rawlings's murderer was the last one to show up, read the sign, and push on. That was all very clear but for one thing. There had been only two pairs of strange outlaws, Ringo and Howard, Rawlings and his killer—name so far unknown. But there had been another two. The ones who had spent the night at this spring. Those two, Perc thought with a sinking sensation, could only be Sam Logan and John Reed, which of course meant they were certainly part of the outlaw gang, were, without much doubt, the ones who had left the mud-daubed arrow on the skull.

He smoked and thought bleak thoughts. Old John Reed hadn't reformed. He'd not only lied to Perc, which is understandable, but he'd also lied to Abbie, and that, in Perc's thoughts, was his most unforgivable sin.

He killed the smoke and reflected upon the northwest country he had yet to traverse to find the rendezvous. He'd hunted all that land and he'd also ridden over it several years before as Snowshoe's rep on the Rainbow roundups. He knew it as well as anyone did, which made it simpler for him to discard a number of secluded places where an outlaw band might come together in secret to plan a series of robberies or divide some loot.

Actually the northward country, nearer the distant mountains and therefore broken and brushy and forested, turned less wild the farther west one traveled because the actual peaks and thrusts swung more to the northeast.

The area where he thought these men might be heading was in fact rather pleasant although it was very isolated. Not only were there no ranches over there but also there was little to draw people this late in the grazing season unless it was the superb hunting and fishing—two things he bleakly doubted any band of renegades would be interested in. On the other hand there were a number of perfect spots for such a rendezvous as he was now convinced was in the making, and whether he followed the murderer of Frank Rawlings or not, he knew them all and could, with luck and a great deal of caution, locate the exact spot.

He left the cottonwood spring and for a while that Cross-Quarter-Circle horse ambled along in his wake, still feeling the gregarious urge of a lonely animal. But as he struck the colt's tracks and neither deviated nor slowed, the Arizona horse dropped steadily to the rear and finally halted, watched him ride on for a while, then turned and started back for the spring and the green grass, the urgent sense of security triumphing over the need for companionship.

He was glad the horse had turned back. Somewhere up ahead Rawlings's killer would undoubtedly take a stand to watch his back trail. Not, Perc knew, because the outlaw thought he was being followed, but simply because it was the second nature of all hunted things—four-legged or two-legged—to observe every instinctive precaution. Survival demanded no less.

But the instincts of the hunter were equally sharp and

cunning. Perc stopped often to scout ahead on foot. Once he saw the outlaw on his Snowshoe colt; the man was drowsing along, all slumped and loose. But another time when he skulked ahead and settled low in among some scrub oaks, the colt was standing, head hung, tied in some *chamizo* brush and his rider was halfway up a rocky slope, sitting like an Indian with his Winchester across his legs, stolidly watching the rearward country.

A prudent tracker never pushed his prey. Perc took his time even when the sun began to drift on down the westward heavens, indicating that unless the outlaw halted soon, Perc would have to, because there would not be sufficient moonlight to track the man after sundown.

Still, this was midsummer, the sun did not completely drop away until nearly 9:00 p.m. Perc had several hours yet to go.

The heat brought fresh thirst. Perc was tempted several times to angle off and go hunt up one of the little waterways in this rolling countryside, but he didn't for the elementary reason that he'd come too far, had gone through too much, to risk losing his man now, this late in the day.

He thought the same thirst that was tormenting him must also drive the outlaw to water. It did, but not until Perc had just about given up the hope that it might. The murderer finally headed straight for a rocky escarpment to the north, which was off his route. Perc knew that spot; evidently the outlaw's horse had smelled the pool of water up there.

He also left his route, but instead of making for the rocky place, he cut back northwestward slightly to come upon another, probably tributary, little pothole where another spring ran year round.

His horse tanked up and would have rolled with the saddle on except that Perc growled at him. Afterward, they rested for a short while in the coolness before stalking onward again toward the place where the outlaw had also watered. Perhaps it was carelessness, perhaps just an inevitable thing resulting from this endless game of cat-and-mouse, but when Perc halted in a stand of spindly pines in response to some instinctive warning, he heard the outlaw up ahead moving in the dry brush.

He froze for a full sixty seconds before dismounting, yanking out his carbine, tying his horse, and sneaking forward on foot. It seemed improbable the outlaw would be bedding down with three or four good daylight hours still ahead of him. Curiosity drove Perc into the low brush where he carefully inched ahead, raising one foot and planting it down silently before lifting forward the other foot. It occurred to him the outlaw might suspect something, might have somehow detected the fact that he was being followed. That suspicion exploded into certainty when a Winchester crashed deafeningly less than a hundred yards southward. He dropped flat when the steely breath of a bullet touched his cheek. Not only had the outlaw somewhere discerned he was being followed, he had also laid a good ambush. He'd ridden to the water hole, left his horse up there, then had slipped back southward with his carbine to wait, and Perc had walked right into the trap.

"That'll learn you," the outlaw snarled, and fired again. "Takes a better man than some damned fool cowboy to stalk me!" He fired his third shot.

Perc was pinned. The brush and grass was bone-dry and rustling-brittle. Any move he made would easily carry to the killer. The only thing in his favor was the fact that after he'd dropped and had not returned the gunfire, the outlaw seemed to quicken with sharply curious interest.

"Hey, cowboy!" he called. "Hey … you there in the brush, fling out your guns!"

Perc didn't move. In fact, he scarcely even breathed. Two of those three bullets had come very close. He knew where his adversary was. The trouble with retaliation was simply that, while he was hidden, his underbrush cover was a long way from being bulletproof. While southward his enemy was securely hidden by a big granite slab that had sometime, in ages past, broken loose from the uphill escarpment and tumbled conveniently out where it was now being used to hide a killer, he lay perfectly motionless with his cocked Winchester ready, but without any intention of firing it. At least not yet.

"Hey, you damned fool!" growled the assassin. "You deaf or something? I said fling out your guns!"

Perc remained like stone. He heard the outlaw's booted feet drag abrasively over shale rock and peered closely down through the dried weeds and arid grass toward the slab of rock, hoping the outlaw would appear in plain view. But he didn't; he obviously was no novice at this kind of fighting. "Cowboy, you hurt …?"

Perc let his breath out very slowly. This is what he'd been waiting for, this was exactly why he hadn't moved.

"You hear me, cowboy, you hit?"

Still Perc lay like dead.

The outlaw mumbled a curse and moved again, behind his slab of granite. Perc heard his gun stock grate over stone as the man inched out where he could peer into the onward tall weeds. He heard the killer curse again as his feet slipped on shale, then that ugly sound of grating wood over unyielding stone came again. But the outlaw wasn't coming up for a look any longer. He was for some reason going back in the opposite direction. It didn't at once occur to Perc what the man was up to, but when it did, he clenched his carbine tighter and swung his head as far as he could to the right.

The outlaw was slipping around where Perc had left his horse.

Whether the man meant to set him afoot or not, he couldn't take the chance, not this far from town and another mount. He braced himself for a very gradual, very gentle movement. Got his free hand set upon the flinty ground and, holding his weight off the dry brush as best he could, gently turned to face in the direction his adversary was now boldly hiking along through the yonder little belt of spindly pines. He glimpsed the man passing through patches of light and shadow, got squared around, raised up into a kneeling position, and snugged back his Winchester. When he had the man across his sights, he hesitated. If he gave the outlaw a chance, the man could—and undoubtedly would—spring behind one of those little trees. If he shot him in cold-blood without giving him any chance to surrender, it would be murder.

He lowered the tip of his carbine, and when next the outlaw stepped between two trees, he fired. The outlaw flung out both arms to catch himself as one leg was violently knocked from under him. He roared a deep-down cry and fell. His Winchester fell ten feet away and hung up in a bush. As the outlaw rolled and wrenched around, Perc stood up and sprang ahead. The man saw him standing there with his carbine, low and ready, less than twenty feet away. He'd been fumbling for his six-gun but now he froze. There was a grotesque angle to the outlaw's left leg below the knee, and a sticky scarlet stain was rapidly spreading to the ground from the shattered leg.

Very slowly the outlaw took his hand away from his holstered .45, made a terrible grimace up at Perc, and made a low, harsh gasp of pain. He was whipped.

Perc stepped over, yanked the man's .45 clear, and threw it away. He set aside his Winchester and kneeled to examine the broken leg.

CHAPTER FIFTEEN

His bullet at that close range had made a gory wound and had broken the man's leg below the knee, but miraculously, perhaps exactly because it had struck at such close quarters, it had made a clean break, and the lead did not shatter, tearing flesh, ligaments, and tendons. Still, it was a very painful injury.

First, Perc tied off the bleeding. Next he cut two straight pine limbs and, using the man's trouser belt, shell belt, neckerchief, and handkerchief, set the bone and lashed the leg so that it was immobile. After that, with dusk settling in under the gloomy big rock cliff above them, he washed at the spring, brought back a hat full of water, and sluiced off the leg and the splint. All through this the evil-faced outlaw had writhed a little and had, from time to time, weakly cursed or gasped, but when it was all over Perc caught the man eyeing his carbine where it had fallen into a bush. Without a word Perc went over, levered the outlaw's gun empty, and brought it back and handed it to the man.

"What's this for?" the outlaw croaked, pale and gray and badly shaken. "It's empty."

"For a crutch," said Perc. He sank down and methodically made a smoke, lit it, pushed it forward, and placed it between his prisoner's eager lips, then made a second smoke for himself. "Before we leave here, mister, you're going to discover that saddle guns make fair crutches."

"Before we …? Where you think you're goin' to take me?"

"To jail down at Ballester."

"You … the law?" the outlaw asked, looking surprised. "Hell, I thought you was just some danged nosy range rider."

"I'm the law, mister. I'm also the man who found your pardner and hauled him into town tied face down across my saddle."

"What you talkin' about," scoffed the prisoner, darkly scowling but also quickly shifting his glance to some indeterminate onward place. "I got no pardner."

"That's right. Not now you haven't. But the night you boys threw down on me in town you had one … an Okie or a Texan … and you shot him in the back south of here at a water hole."

"You're talkin' through the top of your skull," the outlaw growled.

Perc smoked placidly a moment, studied the man's evil, narrow face, raised his booted foot, and set it down upon the man's broken, splinted left leg. The outlaw howled and cursed and started to wrench away. Perc bore down with a little more pressure and took a long drag off his smoke.

"You still say you didn't have a pardner named Frank Rawlings?" he softly asked.

The outlaw choked and gasped. Sweat popped out on his forehead. He rolled his eyes in agony. "I had one," he panted. "All right, Deputy, I had one."

Perc removed his foot and flicked ash. "Tell me about him," he said. "Tell me particularly why you killed him."

The outlaw leaned forward from the waist and placed both hands alongside his broken leg. "Oh, my God," he moaned. "Oh, my God."

Perc smoked and watched, and sat there, waiting. Finally, as the pain eased off, the outlaw leaned far back with his shoulders to a spindly pine and let off a ragged long sigh. He rolled his muddy eyes around at Perc. There was no mistaking the look of slow murder in their depths.

"Start talking," Perc said gently, "and finish your smoke. It'll help."

"Wait until I get into town," the outlaw croaked. "I'll tell the whole cussed world what you just done to me."

"Good idea," said Perc calmly. "Maybe by then you can tell 'em I did it more than once. But when it's your word or mine, mister, and you're a murderer and worse, I sort of doubt you'll get much sympathy around Ballester. Now start talking. Why did you kill Frank Rawlings?"

"Why? Why, because I had to. First off, that crazy idea he had of gettin' you to lock up Sam Logan backfired. You got a real good look at Frank. I told him it was crazy … that it wouldn't work. That you probably already knew Sam was a lawman even if he did shoot a couple of cowboys in your town."

"Naw," growled Perc, dropping his cigarette and grinding it out. "That's not enough to shoot a man in the back over." He reared back and lifted his booted foot. The outlaw's reaction was swift and violent.

"Wait!" he wailed. "Wait, Deputy, I'll tell you, I swear I'll tell you."

Perc lowered his foot and cast a sidelong glance upward. "Hurry up with it," he said, "it's getting late. Be dark directly."

"Well, like I said, I had to kill him." The outlaw paused, considered his mangled leg, and shook his head in anguish. "He was … well, there was some money, you see, an' Frank an' me was to divide it even. But without Frank there'd be twice as much for me, providin' …"

"Providing what?"

"Well. Just providin' …"

Perc sighed, reared back, and raised his foot again. But this time when the outlaw raised both arms in supplicating protest Perc didn't stop. He eased his foot down atop the man's broken leg but he exerted no pressure. All it would take, however, was for him to simply lean forward the slightest bit to cause excruciating agony to rack the murderer again.

"Providing what?" he repeated.

The renegade's eyes were swimming in anticipated agony. He spoke very fast, running all his words together in a breathless rush.

"Providin' the other fellers saw it my way. There was four of us in on it. The other two got the money. We come up here followin' a marked trail, to meet where we'd be plenty safe from detection, to divvy the money and plan our next raid. With Frank out of it, I'd stand to get his share. Now take your damned foot off my leg, please, Deputy."

Perc removed the foot. "Four of you," he said. "What about John Reed and Sam Logan?"

The outlaw looked up. "Reed?" he queried. "John Reed ain't around. There's only Sam Logan ..." Gradually the killer's face underwent a slow change. "Are you tellin' me John Reed's in this somehow, Deputy?"

"Sure he is. He and Sam Logan."

"Logan we knew about because we seen him in the saloon the day we arrived in Ballester. But old John Reed ... hell, Deputy, old John's took the Bible trail. He was down at Wolf Hole in Arizona, preachin' and spoutin' all over the place. He even button-holed me an' Frank one time at the Mormon store down there run by that red-headed lady and liked to shouted us deaf about sin and evilness and all that nonsense. But he was still ..."

Perc, seeing the gradual change come over his prisoner, thought that the mention of John Reed's name was powerful medicine among outlaws.

"Reed's in this, too, mister. Not only in it, but he and Logan are somewhere up in these hills, huntin' for the same meetin' place I'm lookin' for."

The outlaw slumped. He mopped sweat off with a soiled

sleeve. "Frank an' me, we talked about Sam after we seen him in that saloon, Deputy. We got to wonderin' about him being this far north. Last time we seen him was down at Wolf Hole before the robbery at Saint George. Then, all of a sudden, the old devil was here in Ballester. But it was too odd for anythin' but coincidence, Frank said, so we figured to wait until …"

"Until Jim Howard and Charley Ringo got up here, then ask them about it," Perc concluded dryly.

The outlaw nodded. "Yeah. That's about the size of it."

"Ringo got shot in that Saint George robbery, did you know that, mister?"

The outlaw shook his head. "Haven't seen him or Jim since we split up down south and struck out for the Ballester country, ridin' apart, the four of us. How bad?"

"Just through the upper arm. Not bad. Tell me about that robbery."

"Nothin' much to tell. We heard there was a gold shipment comin' through and figured to catch the coach along the ninety-mile deserted stretch of desert between Wolf Hole and Saint George. We did, caught it easy. Only it turned out not to be gold."

"Greenbacks?"

The outlaw nodded. "Damnedest haul of greenbacks you ever saw, Deputy." The outlaw raised his face. For the first time since he'd been shot his expression showed something besides anguish. "Eighty thousand dollars worth of paper currency. Twenty thousand apiece! Deputy, you got any idea how much twenty thousand dollars is, all in one chunk?"

Perc shook his head with complete candor. He had no idea how much money that was, couldn't even adequately imagine. The outlaw's gaze turned crafty, turned speculative. Perc saw this and divined the reason. He said: "Forget it before you even offer me Frank's share to turn you loose. By the way … what's your name?"

"Smith," said the outlaw glibly, but when Perc reared back to take his weight off his booted foot, the outlaw said: "Wait, wait, it's Peter Miller, an' that's the gospel truth. I was born Peter Miller, only I never stuck to it very long. Commenced changin' it every few months right after my seventeenth birthday."

"Where's the meeting place, Pete?" Perc asked.

Miller shook his head and for the first time showed annoyance. "Those damned idiots been leadin' us all over the lousy country with their signs and arrows an' such-like. By God, I've ridden ten times as far already as anyone ought to have to go to get hold of what's rightfully theirs."

Perc eyed the sky and brought his head down slowly. "Sure," he murmured dryly. "What's rightfully yours. Tell me, Pete, how many men got killed when you boys halted that coach?"

"Only two, Deputy. The driver an' the shotgun guard."

"Real considerate of you. Were there any other folks on the coach?"

"No. We figured there would be … you know, to sort of make it appear to be just an everyday run, but there wasn't."

Perc gazed at his captive. If there *had* been passengers, they'd have died, also. That was the usual practice of such murderers as these men when stopping a bullion coach. No witnesses, no identification afterward.

"What's the closest ranch to the spot where you hit that coach, Pete?"

"An outfit called the Cross-Quarter-Circle."

Perc gravely nodded. "They had pretty good horses," he murmured, and stood up. "Where are you wanted besides in Arizona, Pete?"

"Nowhere. Just Arizona."

"How much are you worth?"

"Only five hundred. Listen, Deputy, about Frank's slice of that stack of greenbacks …"

"Pete, I've already told you. You're wasting your breath."

"Well, you figurin' on takin' me back to Ballester tonight?"

Perc didn't answer because this had suddenly become his primary headache and he'd been privately dwelling upon it now for nearly an hour—since he'd shot Miller. If he *did* take the murderer back, he might just as well forget ever catching up with Howard and Ringo. If he didn't, if he went on tracking those other desperadoes, Miller wouldn't be here when he got back … unless … He turned and gazed at that splinted, purple-swollen leg. Unless he took Miller's horse and guns and left him just as he was now, in which case no matter how tough he was or how he struggled, Miller couldn't get very far away by dragging that splinted leg, and even if he could cover a few miles, he'd leave a squiggly track from dragging that leg a blind man could follow.

He made another smoke and lit it. Miller watched him closely. It was clear Perc was turning a number of things over in his mind. It was just as clear to the outlaw, after two abortive attempts, that no outside source could very easily sway Perc's judgment, so Miller wisely kept quiet.

Dusk was settling in fast, especially around this gloomy rock escarpment where the overhead sky was partially blotted out. Fortunately, though, it was warm, would remain warm throughout the night.

A sudden idea struck Perc. He went over, got the Snowshoe colt, brought it back, picked up some of the damp bloody mud where he'd worked over Miller's leg, smeared it generously over the saddle, checked the colt up so that it could not lower its head to graze, and gave it a smart slap across the romp. The startled animal jumped five feet and lit out, running straight southward.

Miller wailed. "What'd you do that for, Deputy? How'd you expect me to get down to Ballester?"

"Fly," said Perc enigmatically, and watched for as long as the running colt was visible. He'd get down to Snowshoe sometime in the night. Johnny and the others would find that bloody saddle,

and, come sunup, they'd come boiling upcountry backtracking the
colt. He turned and walked over beside Miller, kneeled, and shelled
out all the cartridges in the shell belt around the outlaw's broken
leg. Miller watched and tensed, but Perc was gentle. He was also
silent. As he straightened back up, pocketing the bullets Miller
made a puzzled dark frown.

"What in the devil are you up to?" he growled.

Instead of answering Perc retrieved the Winchester, stepped
over, and swung it violently against a tree. Miller let out a squawk
as his gunstock broke into a dozen pieces. Perc tossed the gun down
and faced around. "No guns," he said, "no sting left, Pete. Now tell
me something. Where were you going when you left the swales to
come up here for water?"

"I already told you, damn it, I don't know! There was an arrow
back at a cottonwood spring south and west of here. There was fresh
tracks leadin' in the way that arrow pointed. I followed the tracks.
That's all I know. That was the arrangement Jim and Charley an'
Frank an' I made after the Wolf Hole stage job. We'd come up here.
Charley and Jim knew this country. At least I got that impression
from listenin' to 'em. They'd blaze a trail for Frank an' me."

"They had the money?"

"Yeah. All eighty thousand of it," muttered Miller, and suddenly
looked crestfallen. "Eighty thousand greenbacks …"

CHAPTER SIXTEEN

There was no genuine daylight left when Perc rode away. Dusk, though, was slow turning to darkness in midsummer, so he got back down to the trail Pete Miller had been pursuing before Pete had angled off for water, before night.

But it wasn't enough he saw, as soon as he tried to pick up those tracks Miller had been following. He tried walking ahead, leading his horse, but after a half hour of that the gloom rolled down and silkily blotted everything out.

Still, he kept in the same general direction until a low, fat old boulder loomed up. There, he sat down and made a smoke for supper, told his horse they'd wasted too much time with Miller, and otherwise listened to the hushed night.

After a while the strengthening moon floated up. He killed his smoke and started walking onward leading the horse. He thought briefly of Pete Miller's vehement protests at being left alone back there unarmed and unable to move.

It was one of the interesting things about murderers that, although they could be wholly impersonal about an execution, they couldn't be the slightest bit impersonal about themselves or the reaction of other people to their crimes.

Still, he'd done one charitable thing. He'd left Miller half
his tobacco and half his cigarette papers. If that proved a poor
substitute for food, it was no less than Perc himself was having to
make do with. Furthermore, in his private opinion, it was a lot
more than Miller deserved.

He halted again to consider the onward lay of softly lit land.
There were several rather steep hill slopes discernible ahead. Beyond
them, up through a twisting cañon that grew steeper and gloomier
as it progressed steadily toward wild and tangled uplands, there was
a widening of the trail. He knew all this because he'd once made
a hunting camp on ahead where a creek brawled and tumbled its
southward way down from the yonder peaks.

It did not seem logical to him that the outlaw leaders would persist
until they reached the distant mountains. If they knew this country at
all, they'd know there wasn't any chance at all of discovery up through
the yonder cañon, for even during the grazing season cattle wouldn't
come up in here; it was not only too rocky and steep, it was also too
primitive. There would be meat-eating cougars and bears up in this
wilderness. Their powerful scent would also keep horses out.

Then, he mused, the outlaws must have their rendezvous up in
that spring-watered wide place on ahead. If it wasn't there, he told
his horse as he stepped around to swing up, they'd have to bed down
at the campsite and wait until sunup to pick up the trail again.

He rode on a loose rein, allowing the horse to do its own
picking and choosing. After a while the trail gradually began to
widen as the hillside shoulders curved back and away on both
sides. But, also, there began to be more and more rocks up in here,
tumbled from the northward escarpments perhaps by lightning
strikes or upheavals of the earth in centuries gone. The horse
became very careful in choosing its footing until, a half hour later,
it suddenly lifted its head, shot forward its small ears, and became
quite interested in something it obviously couldn't see, which
meant it had caught a scent.

Again Perc dismounted. This time, as he led the animal along, he kept it up even with him. Should the horse suddenly decide to trumpet a greeting to whatever it had scented on ahead, he could clamp down hard and swiftly, cutting off its wind and thereby also cutting off its noise.

He thought he knew what the beast had scented. Other horses. He also thought he knew who would be riding those other animals. But sometimes when a man's entire being is powerfully concentrating upon a pre-conceived notion, he leaves absolutely no leeway for doubt, and can therefore be more thoroughly wrong than he'd believe possible.

Then he caught the fragrance of a cooking fire. It was definitely coming from that onward grassy clearing where the brawling little white-water creek ran—his old hunting camp. He secured the horse, drew forth his carbine, sniffed a moment to be dead certain about the location of that smell, then started ahead. He hadn't progressed a hundred yards when off on his right up a black, narrow off-shoot cañon a soft sound of crumbling decomposed granite came through to him. He dropped down and raised his Winchester. It was much too dark up that little narrow cañon to see anything, but there was something—man or animal he had no idea—up there.

Only a fool advances against enemies without first making certain his back trail is secure. He waited a long time for that rustling noise to be repeated. It hadn't been a small, nocturnal animal, he was sure of that. After a while it came again, a heavy, shuffling sort of solid movement like a tethered horse would make. It puzzled him. Surely the outlaws wouldn't hide their animals this far beyond their sight. He got up and skulked noiselessly forward. Whatever it was, he had to know before going on around the last bend in the trail on up toward the campsite.

He stepped into the dark, narrow cañon and immediately encountered spiny chaparral that made whispering sounds as it brushed across his lower legs. He paused and strained to see. The moon hadn't yet touched down into this scary place; it was steep-walled and pitch dark. He used the Winchester butt to ease brush aside, took two more steps—and the side of a mountain fell on him. At least that was his reaction to being struck forcibly from off on one side by a mighty weight that drove him backward and sideward until the chaparral, tangling around his legs, upended him back at the mouth of the draw. He dropped his carbine and rolled frantically to get clear of the underbrush. He heard a man's low, deep down growl, thought first it might be a bear, then glimpsed something broad and wraith-like lunging at him.

He rolled again, jackknifed both legs up close, and sprang to his feet. A huge fist sang past his cheek and a hurtling body came at him like a projectile. He whipped sideways and escaped most of that driving force but not all of it. One arm as thick as oak lashed out and struck him across the chest. He dropped straight down as his scarcely visible adversary tried to pivot, tried to catch him before he squirmed away. He came up and spun on the ball of his right foot as he aimed and fired a blasting blow at the other man's middle.

It was like hitting a sack of flour that had been filled to capacity. There was a little give to the flesh, but great corded muscles threw back Perc's fist like they were made of rubber.

He tried again as that writhing, moving, stalking enemy got squared around and planted himself solidly in such a way that Perc couldn't get past and make a run for it back toward his horse. The second punch grated over an upthrown forearm, slid off it overhand, and jarred solidly against hair and bone and gristle. This punch slowed the other man; he seemed just for a second to stagger, to be stunned. Perc, reacting at top speed, sprang sideways to get around the other man. He almost made it, too. He got clear, but when he was dropping down for the next jump a hard, round, coldly impersonal piece of steel came out of the brush at his back and rammed into his side below the ribs. He heard, whoever was holding that gun, cock it.

He froze. A man might sometimes, with luck, escape from a very formidable foeman by thinking lightning fast, but no man living had ever yet outrun or out-dodged a closely aimed bullet. Some had of course tried, but they didn't count because they were no longer among the living.

That silent apparition back in the brush yanked away Perc's six-gun and eased off the hurting pressure of his cocked gun. Then he spoke, and Perc's mouth dropped open. He said: "John, you all right?"

"All right," came the rolling deep-down rumble of John Reed's subdued voice. "But whoever he is, he sure can hit."

Perc slumped. "I thought I'd find you two up here for your share of the eighty thousand," he muttered bitterly.

The gun in his back was withdrawn. The chaparral back there crackled and Sam Logan stepped around to push his face up close and stare. "Be damned," sighed Logan. "John, it's the deputy."

Reed plodded over, planted himself close, too, and also peered. He afterward settled back, gingerly felt his bearded jaw, and said: "Well, Sam, we should've tied him."

"Or you shouldn't have left that note for Abbie, John."

Reed muttered under his breath, wobbled his jaw gingerly, and nodded. Reed put up his gun and handed Perc's .45 back to him. "Squat," he said. Perc squatted. So did Logan, and after a moment more of probing his tender jaw, John Reed also dropped down.

Perc couldn't make out too much in the darkness but he thought both the older men looked and acted dog-tired and disheveled. "Where are your friends?" he quietly asked them.

At once Reed growled: "Keep your voice to a whisper, Deputy. They're on around the bend but that doesn't mean one of 'em might not take a notion to go strolling around."

Sam Logan thumbed back his hat and kept staring at Perc. "You sure got a tough skull," he murmured. "You must've left town about sunup to be here by now."

"I'd have been here sooner but I had a little run-in with Pete Miller."

Both the older men swiftly looked up. Sam said: "Where?"

"A few miles back."

What'd you do with him?"

"Left him there with a splinted broken leg and turned his horse loose."

"His guns," growled John Reed. "Did you leave him his guns?"

Perc shook his head. "No. I took all his slugs and busted his carbine against a tree. I'm going to do the same to you boys, too, the first chance I get."

Logan and Reed exchanged a look. Reed lifted his mighty shoulders and let them slump. "Might as well tell him," he mumbled. "Can't keep him out of our hair anyway, Sam."

Logan nodded and said: "Deputy, you've got some notion we're in on the division of that Saint George stagecoach money. Well, we're not. We were both down there at Wolf Hole, though, when the Howard gang hit the stage and killed those men. John had sent for me to meet him at Wolf Hole after he got out of prison and lit out for Arizona. I went down and met him there, you see, because I was the one who tracked him down years back and sent him to prison. I sort of owed him something, maybe."

"And," stated Reed softly, "you were curious. You see, Percy, Sam and I'd been writing letters back and forth over the years while I was in prison. He wasn't sure I meant it when I wrote him that I'd had enough, that I meant to spend the rest of my life serving the Lord and doing good works."

Logan nodded. "All right. I was curious. Anyway, I rode down, met John and Abbie ... and then we ran across Jim Howard down there with his gang. We also ran onto something else. I was sitting in a saloon at Saint George when Frank Rawlings and this Miller feller took a nearby table and started whispering about the hold-up Howard had planned for his gang. Howard knew me by sight. So did his sidekick, Charley Ringo. But Rawlings and Miller weren't so sure. They're younger men. I'd already retired before they started cutting their teeth on gun barrels. I contacted John and we set out to prevent the hold-up." Logan paused. "We got there too late. Well, I knew where they were heading … to the Ballester country up in Utah … Rawlings and Miller had said as much in that Saint George saloon. I sent word to John, then lit out straight for your bailiwick, Deputy. But it turned out to be a long wait. It seems that there were posses and Army detachments kicking up a big dust all over northern Arizona and southern Utah after that coach was found with the cash gone and the driver and guard shot. So, the members of Howard's gang didn't start drifting in until just a few days ago, and by then, because he came straight through, John had also shown up."

Perc squatted there, looking from one to the other of these rugged older men. Finally he holstered the six-gun Logan had handed back to him and removed his hat, re-creased it, and put it back on. He needed that little space of time to make the necessary mental adjustments to what he'd just been told. He said: "I thought you two were part of the gang. How did you find out where, exactly, this meeting was to take place?"

"I followed Rawlings and Miller," said Logan. "That's why I suddenly disappeared from town and didn't come back until last night when I had to keep you from locking John up … and we put you to sleep. As I've already said, neither Rawlings nor Miller knew me except by sight and reputation. They saw me in the Golden Slipper but they didn't put two and two together, or if they did, they never got to talk it over with Jim Howard. If they had …" Logan dragged a stiff finger across his own throat. "Jim would have known right away what I was up to. He and I've crossed trails before, years back."

Perc looked at the bearded and thickly massive John Reed. "Did you know Ringo and Jim Howard, too?" he asked.

For a moment those piercing pale eyes bored into Perc with a strangely ironic expression in their baleful depths, then the former outlaw ponderously inclined his head. "I knew them boys. I knew them very well. You see, that's partly why I feel it's my obligation to put them out of action. I taught them what they know. Before I was sent away, they were part of the Reed gang."

Perc gazed at these two rough, experienced men whose earlier years had been spent in deadly combat against one another. He stood up and dusted off his breeches. They also stood up. Perc said: "Are you sure Howard and Ringo are on around the bend in that little secret meadow?"

"We're sure," rumbled John Reed. "We'd just come back to fetch our carbines and close in on 'em when you came sneaking in behind us."

Sam Logan picked up Perc's Winchester and returned it to him. "I think you ought to stay out of this," he said quietly, but with a doubtful ring to his words as though he wasn't very hopeful about this. "It's John's job and my job. It's been coming a long time, Perc, been coming toward this final showdown many years. We'd like to finish it ourselves. It's been a long trail for us … very long. It's probably our last trail, too."

Perc gazed at their lined old faces, thought a moment of their violent, fierce lives, and smiled at them. "Sure enough," he murmured. "You're the bosses. I'll just sort of back your play."

Even John Reed smiled now. "Good boy," he whispered. "Good boy. I told Abbie … well, never mind what I told Abbie." Reed looked around for his dropped carbine, found it, brushed dust and leaves off it, and looked gloweringly over at his smaller companion. "Good luck, Sam," he said. "You're going to need it. I taught those two well."

Logan's long upper lip drew back in a slow, mirthless grin. "But not well enough," he said evenly. They all knew what he was thinking. He'd beaten the notorious John Reed at the height of Reed's violent career, so he'd be a match for Reed's lieutenants.

Reed swung half around and was quiet for a while as he looked over where the onward trail was faintly visible now because that moon was nearly overhead. "Keep a close watch anyway, Sam. Charley'll be half out of it with that hurt right arm, but Jim ..." Reed solemnly wagged his bushy head. "Jim's as good with guns as I was at his age."

Perc stepped around them to walk on up the trail. Logan hissed at him. "Hold it, son. That's not the way. You just stay back here with us. We'll give you a little useful educating."

Perc halted, waited for the older men silently to pace on up, then he stayed with them as far as the last curve before they'd have walked out into the yonder wide place where notorious Jim Howard and Charley Ringo had a little dying campfire. There, without a word, Reed took to the left slope, Sam took to the right, and Perc went with the smaller man up into the gloomy, sharp rocks beside the trail.

CHAPTER SEVENTEEN

It was the flickering light they saw first. It came from the center of an ancient stone ring over beside the white-water creek. Perc had also used that stone ring. It was black with age and smooth from the heat of many cooking fires. He now recalled the last time he'd camped up here while on a hunting trip when he'd been riding for Snowshoe, that he'd thought probably that generations of Indian hunters had also used that same fire ring.

What he'd never imagined in his wildest dreams back in those less burdensome days was that sometime he'd be silently scaling the westward slope under such bizarre circumstances, stalking the two most wanted outlaws in the West, in this identical spot, with a pair of companions as improbable, as unbelievable, as anyone could have imagined.

Sam Logan paused and scowled when Perc's right foot grated over stone. It had been a scarcely audible sound, but the wiry little lawman had disapproved of even that much noise. Perc stopped and looked carefully where he'd put his next few steps, picked out the most unyielding places, and nodded. Sam went on again, moving with agonizing slowness up the side hill, sometimes pausing for long periods, sometimes silently gesturing toward a place where treacherously loose shale lurked.

They climbed until they could gaze straight down into the secret place. There were two horses down there, full of grass and water and standing like stone with their heads down. There were also two bedrolls not far from the dying little fire, and near the bedrolls two flung-down saddles with their saddlebags detached and lying near some soiled tin dishes and cups beside the fire.

But there were no men.

Perc found a level, wind-swept ledge, belly-crawled out upon it, and gradually let all the stiffness and wariness leak out. When Sam Logan came down and eased out his full length, also, Perc whispered to him.

"Did you see them when you scouted up the place before?"

Sam intently studied the meadow for a long moment before nodding and saying in a low whisper. "Saw Charley. He was at the creek, washing his hurt arm. Didn't see Jim, but he's there. They're both down there. Maybe John can see 'em from over across the pass."

Perc reared up slightly to look across at the opposite jumble of dark, jagged rock where John Reed had faded out when they'd split up. It was possible that from over there John had a better view of the entire meadow, at least of that part of it that was directly below where he undoubtedly now was quietly lying. His attention was rudely yanked back to the meadow when Sam Logan laid a vice-like set of steely fingers on Perc's arm and squeezed. Logan said nothing but he was intently staring down into the little meadow.

A burly man came ambling out of the northward night where black basalt and dark trees added to the total gloominess of that northwestward rim.

"Charley," breathed Sam Logan, watching this man's approach toward the dying little fire.

Ringo was the one Doc Farraday had treated. Perc still had a folded Wanted poster with Ringo's likeness upon it in his shirt pocket, and although he recognized the face without much difficulty, he'd never before seen Ringo as he now saw him, walking up to the fire, tall and thickly set up, unkempt and vicious-looking.

The outlaw kicked up some sparks with his boot toe, squatted down, and began making a cigarette beside the fire. It was a warm night and therefore it was only habit that had driven the outlaw to the fire. He poked around in the coals, picked up a red ember, lit up, and exhaled. He twisted half around and gazed directly behind himself over where a meandering trail led on out of this little hidden place. Perc knew that trail well; it led up into the higher, rougher country where there was good hunting.

But these men were not here for the hunting, as Ringo demonstrated when he called softly saying: "Jim, forget it. No need to hide it anyway. They're not comin'."

For a while there was no sign of anyone over by the yonder pass, then the second man strolled forward. He was just as tall and just as thickly made as Ringo was, but with a noticeable difference. Jim Howard walked balanced forward on the balls of his feet like a fighter or a wary wolf. He moved, even now when he was confident of being perfectly safe, with a quick, thrusting stride, his head constantly moving, his eyes seldom still. Perc was impressed—the most notorious lawbreaker he'd run up against so far down in Ballester had been a one-time horse thief. Otherwise, his arrests usually were prosaic enough: Boots for getting tanked to the eyeballs, or some other cowboy who wanted to bay at the moon.

But this man he was watching now was totally different from anything he'd encountered before. He began to have serious doubts of his ability to handle those two if he'd come onto them alone. Very serious doubts. Often enough cowboys took up deputy's badges, but facing a man whose decade-long renegade career had turned him into a walking machine of deadly destruction was something cowboy deputies were rarely ever called upon to interfere with, or if they tried, they died.

"That," announced Sam Logan quietly, "is Jim Howard."

"Looks rough," Perc whispered, not looking away as Howard walked over and joined Ringo at the fire.

"Deadliest man with guns you'll ever see," responded Logan, also studying the pair of big, heavily armed men down there at the fire. "Deadliest pair in the business today."

"What're you figuring on doing?"

"It's John's play," stated Logan. "That's what he wants and that what we'll wait for."

Ringo growled from beside the fire with his face screwed up against the rising tobacco smoke. "They'd have made it by now. The trail was plenty plain even for those two dumbheads."

Howard yawned and stretched, then slumped. "Twenty thousand each," he said in a low, deep voice. "I thought we were crazy to make this rendezvous anyway. Figured right after we split up you and me should've headed west out to California and let them two poke around up here, lookin' for us while we was raisin' a little hell out at Frisco."

Ringo smoked and eyed the embers at his feet and shrugged. He obviously didn't care one way or another.

"How long you want to wait?" Howard asked.

"Too dark to light out now. Might as well hang around until morning … then head out."

"Which direction?"

Ringo looked around and lifted his lips in a wolfish grin. "West. Out Frisco way."

Howard held out his right hand. "Give me some tobacco," he said, and the minute Ringo laid the papers and sack in his palm, Perc felt Sam Logan stiffen beside him. It didn't dawn on Perc right away why Sam had done that. By the time it did dawn on him, a bull-bass rumbling voice rolled out over the downhill meadow like distant cannons. John Reed had made his play. He'd waited with Indian-like patience until the only uninjured gunhand down there between those two deadly killers was too occupied to streak for a gun.

"Freeze, Jim!" boomed out John Reed from some invisible place up in the northward rocks. "You, too, Charley. Freeze and stay froze. One flicker of an eyelash and you'll both go to hell!"

Perc watched those two burly men down there. They seemed taken not only by total surprise, but they also seemed stunned with recognition of that unmistakable booming old voice thundering down at them. Howard still had his right hand extended. He'd just started to close the fingers around Ringo's tobacco sack, had just started to draw the hand back, when that clap of thunder had struck him.

Ringo, too, didn't move so much as a muscle. He was staring from widened eyes in the general direction Reed had spoken from. It was Ringo who recovered from the shock first, but he still didn't move.

"John," he said, "is that you up there? John Reed …?"

"That's right, Charley," rumbled Reed. "It's I. I've come for the pair of you … murderers, butchers, thieves, animals. I've come for the pair of you!"

Finally Jim Howard recovered and said: "Yeah, we're everything you say we are, John. But we got eighty thousand dollars. How much *you* got?"

That booming voice rolled out through the hills again saying: "Sam, go down and disarm 'em. Percy, stay where you are. Shoot if one of them so much as flexes his fingers."

Howard and Ringo turned their heads a little and rolled their eyes when Sam Logan rose up, no longer trying to be quiet, and started slipping and sliding down toward the little meadow.

Ringo said: "Sam? Sam *Logan?*"

"The same!" roared old John Reed. "Sam Logan and John Reed serving the good cause now, you two carrion. You know Sam, so if you want to make a break, now's the time. You wait any longer and Sam'll make mincemeat out of you."

Perc was fascinated. This was more than a capture. It was something violent and twisted and steeped in fierce hatred among these men. There was none of the usual disgust or contempt, none of the sulkiness of the vanquished or the stiff triumph of the victors; these men knew each other very well, had known each other a long time; they could talk back and forth as they were now doing without anything between them such as had lain between Perc and Pete Miller back there, because only one thing lay between these men. Not being captured or being vanquished, but death pure and simple. Someone was going to die here. Perc knew it as surely as he knew his own name. Among these four there was no such thing as surrender. There was only death.

"You're a fool, John!" called out Jim Howard. "You're an old man. You got a girl to look after. Twenty thousand dollars would set you up in clover for life. How about those years in prison, John? You want to get paid for them, too? Just swivel that gun up there and center it on Sam. We'll hand you twenty thousand cash … and a ten thousand dollar bonus for killin' Sam."

"Scum," rumbled John Reed from his hiding place up the northward slope. "I had in mind trying to save your souls when I first came up here, Jim, but it's been borne in upon me since I been here that you two've got no souls to save. You're worse than animals. You didn't have to kill that driver or that guard. I taught you different years back. You're not worth saving, either one of you."

Sam got all the way down into the meadow. The pair of killers saw him and stared over at him. Neither they nor Sam Logan said a word but John Reed's rumbling denunciations rolled on and on.

To Percy, with his carbine pushed ahead and ready, it was uncanny; it wasn't like any showdown he'd ever heard of before. Sam started forward toward the motionless killers. He moved slowly and thoughtfully, never once putting himself between John Reed's gun muzzle and their captives. Finally, as he inched around behind the bigger men, Sam said: "You're the only two I'd have made this trip for, boys. You're the only two I'd have come out of retirement for." He removed Ringo's gun, stepped back, and flung it over into the creek.

He was in no hurry about any of this. Perc got the definite impression neither of these old hell-raisers wished to conclude this meeting in a hurry. "You'll also have a boot knife," he said to Ringo's back. "And a belly-gun. Bend over, Charley, and shed the knife first."

Jim Howard strained up toward Reed's place of concealment, his neck muscles standing out with fury. "Twenty thousand for Sam dead!" he called. "Forty thousand, John. Half for Sam dead, half for lookin' the other way when we ride out of here. John! Use your head! That's more money than you ever got in one job, and this here'll be legal money. We own it. We'll give you half."

"Legal money," snorted Reed. "Blood money, Jim. I've told you a dozen times … never kill unless you have to."

While these two bawled back and forth, Charley Ringo bent down, lifted his right pants leg, fished out a wicked-bladed knife, and tossed it away. He then, with Sam's urgings sounding softly from behind, fished under his shirt and brought forth a big-bored little .41 Derringer double-barrel that he also tossed away.

"That's all," he said, and called Sam Logan a bad name. "I should've killed you ten years ago, Sam. But it's not too late now."

Perc had been waiting for this. He'd known from the beginning it was coming, but still, when Ringo started to move, Perc was caught not quite prepared. Ringo whirled with surprising speed for a large man, roared a curse, and hurled himself straight at smaller and lighter Sam Logan. It was a terrible mistake, for if Ringo had counted on Sam's chivalry about not shooting an unarmed man, he'd just lost the biggest bet of his lifetime.

CHAPTER EIGHTEEN

Logan's red-flaming muzzle blast was partially muffled by big Charley Ringo's body when he fired pointblank. Ringo's head jarred forward, his hat flew off; he jack-knifed into an almost bent-double position when that big slug struck him, and he staggered one more step forward before the total impact halted him in his tracks.

Sam Logan hadn't moved an inch. He didn't move now, with Ringo dying at his feet, until the bigger man began to roll forward in a face-down fall. Then Sam sprang clear.

Perc hadn't been able to fire even though he'd seen Ringo's desperate charge coming, because Sam was too close. It didn't matter now. Charley Ringo was dead before he hit the ground.

But the gunshot, the bull-like howl Ringo had made just before he'd been killed, gave Jim Howard all the room he'd needed. He flung down the little tobacco sack in his right hand, dropped low, and went for his .45 at the same time he whirled away.

Reed fired from up in the rocks but Perc still didn't dare fire because now Sam was moving, crab-like, to the side and swinging to shoot it out with deadly Jim Howard.

Reed's first shot missed wide. He bawled out a thunderous warning to Logan to which Sam did not pay the slightest heed, and fired again.

That time Reed's bullet tore the brim of Howard's hat, leaving the gunman bareheaded but still concentrating fully upon Sam Logan.

Howard, as Perc saw without breathing, was lightning fast with his gun. He had it out and tilting upward before Sam had struck down over where he'd jumped away from Ringo's falling body.

Then Perc saw an amazing thing happen. Sam's gun with its fancy mother-of-pearl handle was in his right hand. As he hit the ground after jumping away from Ringo's tumbling body, he fired once, flipped the gun into his opposite hand to clear Ringo's fall, and fired again with scarcely any interlude between those two shots. It had, in a way, been not unlike the famous border-shift some expert gunfighters used, but under these circumstances is was even more daring because Sam had to have been thinking faster than the gun was firing to allow that fraction of a second to pass between the time Ringo stumbled forward and the time he got off those two shots. Perc was staggered by such gunmanship.

Jim Howard was also staggered, but from something a lot more lethal and damaging than a vision of unexcelled speed and forethought. Both of Sam's bullets struck Howard. He dropped backward from the impact but did not fall. Up in the rocks John Reed was no longer shooting. Perc, still unable to risk a shot for fear of striking Logan, was also silent. The entire battle now hinged upon which of two of the deadliest gunmen in the West should get off the next shot.

But no other shot was ever fired.

Howard tried. He had his mouth open, his neck muscles corded from the effort, and his slumping body fighting with every resource left to it. But that weighted-down right hand could only raise a few inches; it was rapidly turning numb. Howard's co-ordination was slipping away fast. He gasped and strained until his eyes bulged from the effort. Still his gun arm would not come high enough. The leaden weight of the heavy six-gun kept it hanging too low, too useless, for him to get off his shot.

Sam stood like stone, waiting, watching, his own gun cocked

and dead-leveled. But he did not pull the trigger. He could have. He could've drilled Jim Howard through the heart or the head. He didn't. He watched the dying man without flinching or firing. When Howard sobbed an unsteady curse and his fingers gradually opened to let his gun fall, Sam Logan eased off the hammer of his own .45, dropped the weapon into his holster, and straightened up to his full, slightly less than average height.

"Take it easy," he said softly to Howard. "It's all over … take it easy, Jim."

John Reed was scrambling down out of the rocks making enough noise to be heard a long way off. Perc took his cue from the older man and also got up to start hastily down into the meadow. Both of them got down and trotted over to where the loathsome stench of burned gunpowder was very strong.

Howard was down in a sitting position with both hands clasped across his middle where a welter of shiny wetness was oozing around his clenched fingers. He looked blankly at Perc, looked up at John Reed, and said: "You lousy old turncoat, John. I should've killed you the first day I laid eyes on you down in Arizona."

Sam Logan was down on one knee beside the dying man. "A heap of things all of us should've done different, Jim," he murmured. "Rest easy. You want a smoke?"

Howard turned his head heavily and regarded Logan. "That was a good switch," he muttered. "Sam, I always said there was only one man on this stinkin' earth who just might beat me with guns. You."

"Perc," muttered Logan. "Make him a cigarette."

Perc went to work with the last of his tobacco. As he did this, he said: "Howard, Pete Miller killed Frank Rawlings while Frank was lying down drinking at a water hole. Shot Frank in the back." He finished the cigarette, lit it, and stuck it between Howard's gray, slack lips. "I ran onto Miller tracking you fellows up here this afternoon, broke his leg, disarmed him, and left him at a water hole. Thought you'd want to know."

Howard closed his eyes and seemed to have trouble lifting the leaden lids again. "Sure, Deputy," he muttered, and drew in a shaky breath. "Rawlings is no loss. Neither is Miller. But Charley is ... Charley was a pretty good man ... Sam?"

"Yeah, Jim?"

"Charley used to say he'd kill you someday because you wouldn't pot an unarmed man. Used to say he'd let you disarm him, then kill you with his hands ... Sam?"

"I'm here, Jim."

"Charley sure guessed wrong, didn't he?"

"Yeah, he guessed wrong, Jim. Where'd you put the money, over in the rocks across the meadow?"

"Yeah. Buried it under some rocks an' leaves ... John, you old Bible banger, you ... We were pretty good friends in the old days, weren't we?"

"Yes," rumbled Reed. "Don't worry about it, Jim. I'll say the right words for you."

Perc saw the cigarette smoke drift up. He also saw the milkiness of Jim Howard's dying stare. He said: "Sam ... John ... he's dead."

Neither of the older men moved. They exchanged a look that Perc couldn't fathom. He got up and turned to go back after their horses. He wanted of a sudden to get away from this place, to get down out of these dark, brooding hills. The still warm air seemed suffocating to him. He walked swiftly out where they'd all left their animals, got the beasts, and stood in total darkness beyond the little meadow for a while deeply breathing and allowing those four older men in there, two dead, two alive, to do whatever such men did at their last rendezvous. Then he took the horses back into the meadow and found John Reed standing with his fierce old beard tilted skyward, silently praying over the two bodies at his feet.

Sam Logan was over across the little meadow, scuffling in the rocks. He'd twisted up a dry-grass torch and was using it to see by. Perc went over to help but he needn't have. Logan had found the freshly turned earth and rocks without any trouble and was holding up a sweat-stiff saddlebag that looked insignificant enough until he opened it and the wild, swirling light shone in upon all that crisp money.

"Eighty thousand dollars," Logan mused, and handed the bag to Perc as he dropped his torch and stamped on it. "Deputy, did you ever wonder what a man's life is worth?"

Perc did not answer. He buckled the saddlebag closed and flung it across his shoulder. Over across the clearing where a dying fire sullenly glowed, John Reed was calling his God to witness the passing of two outlaws. Logan raised his head and also gazed over there.

"For those two," Logan continued in the same vein as before, "their lives were worth forty thousand dollars each. For the two harmless men they murdered on the road between Wolf Hole and Saint George … their lives weren't worth any more than a couple ounces of lead would bring. Sometimes it makes a man wonder, doesn't it?"

They walked back over and silently bent to hoist Charley Ringo over a horse. They then bent and heaved Jim Howard over another saddle. Perc looked at the brands of these animals that Sam Logan had caught and rigged out in Perc's absence. Two more Cross-Quarter-Circle horses. He shook his head, said nothing, and fell to making the bodies fast on one side while Logan also wordlessly worked on the other side. When they finished, John Reed went over to the creek, washed his hands and face, and continued to kneel for a little while, until Sam softly called to him, then old John got upright and walked back.

"The last trail," John said to Sam Logan. The ex-lawman gravely inclined his head and gave Reed look for look. "I've got a vexing question in my mind, Sam," went on the massive ex-outlaw. "Why did you keep getting between me and Jim?"

"Just didn't think, I reckon," muttered Logan, and turned toward his own horse.

"Sam!"

Logan halted and turned back. Again those two gravely considered one another.

"No, Sam," rumbled Reed. "Maybe you could tell Perc that. Or anyone else. But not me ... remember? We know each other too well. Tell me why you did it, Sam."

"What difference does it make," growled Logan. "It's like you just said ... our last trail. It's over and done with."

"The acts are over, Sam, but the memories will never be over for any one of us who was here. Why, Sam?"

Logan's brows dropped straight down. "You're beginning to make me mad," he told Reed. Then he said, with a rough shrug: "All right. You want the record set straight and the memory cleared up. Because, John, it doesn't look right ... a parson killing even renegades like those two. With me it's different. I figure something like this as a duty. It'd never give me a sleepless night or a moment of remorse. I did it so you not only couldn't shoot 'em, but also so's you wouldn't even dare try. You want a new life as a man of the Lord. I just handed it to you, John. Now let's get the hell out of here."

Logan mounted up, bent to catch the reins of Jim Howard's horse, and rode on. He kept his face averted from both Perc and John Reed as he started ahead.

Perc mounted next and took Charley Ringo's beast in tow. The last of them to heave himself up over leather and ride wearily out of the meadow with its stillness and its dying little red-glowing fire was John Reed.

The only time either of the older men spoke after that, until they reached town again, was when Sam Logan twisted and said to Perc: "Where'd you leave that other one?"

Perc took the lead after that and kept it until they found Pete Miller. He hadn't moved; his leg was terribly swollen, and he was in agony. They piled him unceremoniously atop one of the horses carrying the dead men and resumed their way.

Along toward sunup Perc, in the lead again, spotted a band of hard-riding men racing upcountry toward them. "That'll be Johnny West and his Snowshoe men," he told the others, and proved he was correct when the cowboys slid their horses a half mile out and sat like stone as the living men went on past, leading the dead and injured men.

Johnny would have spoken to them but Perc looked straight over at West and shook his head. The Snowshoe men let them ride on. Only old Boots glared at Perc and moved his lips. None of the others had a single word to say.

The sun was well up by the time they came within sight of Ballester. The usual powder-fine sprinkling of dust was beginning to rise up down there where people were beginning to stir, to brace themselves for the rigors of another summertime hot day.

Perc hung back until he was riding between the pair of older men. He said: "Parson, about that church meeting …tomorrow's Sunday again. I'll spread the word." He watched John Reed's red-rimmed tired eyes soften a little. "And about leaving town … forget it. Ballester needs a church. More than that, it needs a good parson."

"Even though he was once a jailbird and before that …?"

"Maybe," broke in Perc quietly, "that's exactly the kind Ballester needs, Parson. I don't reckon a man's ever been very successful fighting the devil until he's once known him. Wouldn't you say so, Sam?"

Logan nodded and slowly smiled. "For a thick-skulled young buck, Deputy, you got a pretty fair set of brains on you at that. You're plumb right."

"It takes a lot of money to build God's house in the wilderness, Perc," rumbled old John Reed, looking solemn as they came near the west side of town.

"You've got enough, Parson. About twenty-five hundred dollars ought to do it, hadn't it?"

Both Logan and Reed looked closely at Perc. Neither of them seemed to grasp what he was talking about. He told them.

"Miller's worth five hundred from Arizona. Jim Howard's worth at least three times that in different places. Ringo's worth about as much as Howard. The only one I don't think has got a price on him was Rawlings. He hardly counts anyway. It's all yours, Parson. Build us a church here in town and maybe buy yourself a little house in town to boot."

Sam Logan bent and peered around Perc at the bearded, burly man on Perc's far side. "There you are," he said with strong emphasis. "I never heard of reward money being put to half as good a use, John. What say?"

Reed was silent a long while. They were passing in behind the nearest houses before he raised a massive fist and dug at his eyes with it. "Dust in the air," he growled a trifle unsteadily. "The Lord's will be done, boys. The Lord's will be done. We'll raise up our church here, and we'll use it to remind others where waywardness leads. You've convinced me."

Perc left Logan and John Reed, made his way out back to Doc Farraday's place, routed out the medical man, and left him with two corpses and an outlaw with a broken leg. Before Farraday got over his initial surprise, Perc turned and loped on down the alleyway past the Reed wagon to Ab Fuller's livery barn. There, he left his tucked-up horses with orders for Ab to give them the best of everything, then he headed straight over to the boarding house for a bath, a shave, some clean clothes, and then a return trip to the Reed wagon to have a talk with Abbie.

A lot of things had happened, but as is the way with life all of them were concluded, all that remained were some loose ends—and the future. Abbie, he promised himself, was going to be part of that future, or his name wasn't Perc Whittaker.

THE END

ABOUT THE AUTHOR

Lauran Paine who, under his own name and various pseudonyms has written over a thousand books, was born in Duluth, Minnesota. His family moved to California when he was at a young age and his apprenticeship as a Western writer came about through the years he spent in the livestock trade, rodeos, and even motion pictures where he served as an extra because of his expert horsemanship in several films starring movie cowboy Johnny Mack Brown. In the late 1930s, Paine trapped wild horses in northern Arizona and even, for a time, worked as a professional farrier. Paine came to know the Old West through the eyes of many who had been born in the 19th Century, and he learned that Western life had been very different from the way it was portrayed on the screen. "I knew men who had killed other men," he later recalled. "But they were the exceptions. Prior to and during the Depression, people were just too busy eking out an existence to indulge in Saturday-night brawls." He served in the U.S. Navy in the Second World War and began writing for Western pulp magazines following his discharge. It is interesting to note that all of his earliest novels (written under his own name and the pseudonym Mark Carrel) were published in the British market and he soon had as strong a following in that country as in the United States. Paine's Western fiction is characterized by strong plots, authenticity, an apparently effortless ability to construct situation and character, and a preference for building his stories upon a solid foundation of historical fact. ADOBE EMPIRE (1956), one of his best novels, is a fictionalized account of the last twenty years in the life of trader William Bent and, in an off-trail way, has a melancholy, bittersweet texture that is not easily forgotten. In later novels like THE WHITE BIRD (1997) and CACHE CAÑON (1998), he showed that the special magic and power of his stories and characters had only matured along with his basic themes of changing times, changing attitudes, learning from experience, respecting Nature, and the yearning for a simpler, more moderate way of life.